A Convenient Sacrifice

Butterton Brides Book 1

Ann Elizabeth Fryer

Copyright © 2023 by Ann Elizabeth Fryer

All rights reserved.

No portion of this book may be reproduced in any form without written permission from the publisher or author, except as permitted by U.S. copyright law.

This is a work of fiction. Similarities to real people or events are entirely coincidental

This book is lovingly dedicated to
Josephine Lohr,
In honor of her high school graduation.
For her romantic spirit,
Sensitive heart,
And strong character.
A true heroine of her own story.

Chapter One

October 17, 1809

Icy rain bit at my cheeks as I exited Lord Sherborne's carriage. He was to meet us here. My eyes followed the height of the church steeple, its sacrificial cross pierced the sky. Unlike this spire, my duty would never be seen by public eyes. Twas incomparable and unknown.

Aunt Honora squeezed my hand. "For such a time as this…" Yet another reminder.

Sacrifices were to be expected. My own small cross would be invisible to the world—I must keep it tucked within the folds of my spirit, must shoulder it in silence. I still did not know what to make of the sudden changes that had come over my life. The one thing I could latch onto was, indeed, my duty. This I would perform. I'd give my life for it—so others might survive.

But would I?

A cutting wind sliced through our cloaks as the church doors opened and quickly closed behind us. A cold day for a wedding. My heart may never warm again. My brother limped to my side, solemn and grave. The deep cuts to his face had not healed. He nudged me forward. And pushed yet again. Did I appear hesitant? With six little mouths to feed, my darling nieces and nephews—I clapped a hand to my mouth, my eyes blurred. I wouldn't see them for a very long time.

Aunt Honora pulled a handkerchief from her sleeve. "Quick about it, dear. Don't let Lord Sherborne see you dismayed." This matter must not be questioned. Clearly.

There, in the shadowy cove at the front of the church stood the baron I would wed. The kind rector hovered beside him, his white vestments ghostlike. A darker autumn day London had not seen. Few candles had been lit, so I couldn't see Lord Sherborne's expression. Did he regret his decision? A part of me wished he did. Perhaps he'd see how pale I'd become in the aftermath of the disaster and change his mind. Choose to cast my family away to poverty. But that couldn't happen.

My brothers had lost everything. One, his life, the other, his livelihood. Poverty crouched at our door like a beast. There'd be no one else to save the Dawes family. Not since Father had speculated years prior, not since—my breath caught. I was at the altar. Aunt Honora left my side—an empty chasm spread when I most needed support and warmth.

Lord Sherborne's glacial blue eyes pierced mine as though the sacrifice were his alone. My redeemer towered above me, brooding and dark. He claimed the fault of our near-poverty and thereby claimed a cure. By claiming me as his.

I trembled from cold, from apprehension. And fear. I wondered why such a man needed me. Why, if my family's disaster was his fault, did the cure require marriage? But no other recompense had been offered. My hand only would save them. This marriage in exchange for their care and sustenance.

He'd made the arrangements with Carl and Aunt Honora. I received his marriage offer by letter. They insisted this was a remarkable boon to my life. His generosity beyond measure. As the wife of a baron, my place in society would be restored. As though I cared for society after my lifelong friends had abandoned me. Left me alone.

The minister began to speak, I scarcely heard. I startled when Lord Sherborne took my hands into his, their gloved presence doing nothing to prevent the pounding of my heart. I could not meet his gaze.

Aunt Honora's words came back to me. "If you'd been one of your brothers, you surely would have died on the ship with the others. If you'd been but a girl, you could not marry. But you are neither. You are Elaina Dawes, aged twenty-and-two, born to save our family."

She'd taken my face between her lace-gloved hands, her loving eyes wet with tears. "Our own Queen Esther. For such a time as this…" No small task.

Lord Sherborne shifted and I realized I'd been holding my breath. Vows. The rector recited those beautiful, age-old words meant for those who deigned to pledge love. I repeated them, the taste of those words like a fine wine never to be savored. I vowed myself to this man so that my family could have housing and bread. Could survive.

Lord Sherborne's vows flowed down to me. His voice, strong and certain, repeated the words as though nailing them in place. An unchanging covenant. Forever.

It made no sense, why a baron of means would stoop to marry a woman of reduced circumstances. My sister began the ruination of our family before Father lost his extensive holdings. Her elopement had been a foreshadowing of the Dawes family's decline. Next Father died, followed by Mother. My brothers took on the shipping business, forged by the generosity of patrons and friends—who would never see a return on investments made.

Lord Sherborne spoke again. "With this ring I thee wed, with my body I thee worship, and with all my worldly goods I thee endow: In the Name of the Father, and of the Son, and of the Holy Ghost. Amen."

I held my breath again.

He removed the glove from my left hand and I caught the quirk of his lips as he slipped a ring onto my finger. An oval ruby surrounded by simple gold caught a flash of candlelight. Deep and red, like the depths of one's heart.

"I now pronounce you man and wife..."

He held my hand observing the glimmer, then bade me to face him. "Lady Sherborne..." He hesitated. Struggled. "We must hasten."

He guided me to the register and we signed our names. The last time I'd be able to write Elaina Dawes—now Lady Sherborne...a name I'd taken as my own. For as long as I lived. Such a strange sound, to be called by another's name.

He offered his arm and escorted me away from the well-wishing rector. I slipped from his grasp and wrapped my arms around Aunt Honora but she turned me back and curtsied.

"God go with you, dear. I wish you well." The bonnet strings beneath her chin quivered.

Carl stood nearby. I'd said goodbye to my sister-in-law last evening. Hugged the children and read them one final story. He nodded. "Elaina..." The wound above his eye was deep and black with thread, the other would leave a trail of claw-like scars down his handsome face. Perhaps it was true that the Dawes family would be marred beyond repair, despite my inalterable union.

I caught a look that passed between him and Lord Sherborne. Carl nodded again. Too grieved to be happy. I suspected contentment would be a long time in coming to any of us. Not after what had happened.

We passed through the doorway outside. A darker shadow descended as icy rain pelted the ground.

Lord Sherborne held my elbow as we descended the steps. "We must away."

My trunks had already been lashed to the back of the waiting coach. A footman held the door open. Away...away... Would I ever return? To myself? Back to the way things were? Impossible.

We dashed into the carriage, Lord Sherborne handed me inside and climbed to the opposite seat. The door shut, and I was jerked forward into an entirely new existence. I've never heretofore experienced the clutch of fear that wrapped my middle. Not even when I learned the Zephyr crashed against the smuggler's rocks had the terror overwhelmed me. Of course, by then, the event was a few days old.

I did not know the baron very well. He'd been scarce about Town the one season I'd enjoyed. Carl assured me of his good character, Aunt Honora too, but swiftly reminded me that I couldn't be particular in the case of poverty. She had pursed her lips at my further inquiry and shook her head. She knew something but didn't tell me. Whatever it was surely wouldn't change the course of my future.

I'd scarcely ever been alone in the presence of a man. Lord Sherborne leaned back in his seat, removed his gloves and tucked them into his coat. Dare I ask the obvious? Dare I beg to know his motives?

I trembled at the thought of forcing a confession.

"You are cold." He pulled a blanket from beneath his seat and handed it to me. I took it, grateful for the soft shield. If only I might hide completely.

I could ply him now and not spend years wondering. I'd enter this marriage with a full knowledge rather than the deep ambiguity I felt. I wrapped the green wool around me and plunged ahead with my query.

"Why did you marry me?" My voice scraped weakly.

He trapped my eyes with his. The murky clouds were nothing to the black shock of hair and brow that towered above me. "You did not deserve your impending fate."

I twisted the blanket in my hands. "I daresay you did not cause it..." What part of the truth had been withheld from me?

"Depends on how you look at it."

"My brother says—"

One of his dark brows lifted. "Go on. What does your brother say?"

Carl had said many things. I suddenly couldn't sort it out, not with Lord Sherborne looking at me as though I were Carl, and he—I don't know. "He says that no one could have predicted the outcome."

"But someone did predict the outcome."

"I don't understand."

"You have suffered a great loss." He curved the conversation, reminding me of the grief that nipped at my heels. Trevor had only been buried a fortnight. My fourteen-year-old nephew, Matthew, never washed ashore.

In a blink, my funerary clothes had been changed to wedding attire. Despite the freezing rain and tears that yet stained our faces, Aunt Honora insisted I wear a thin, pale-yellow gown, better fit for an evening at Almacks on a warm day than a brief wedding that would end with a swift escape to Sherborne's estate.

What did he mean—I didn't deserve my fate? "Rain falls on the just and the unjust." Words I repeated from the funeral.

He claimed my eyes again. "Have you been unjust?"

"I hope not."

"I know you have not."

How could he? Did he spy on me as a fly upon the wall?

He continued our talk of rain. "Then it is my duty to shelter the just." He nodded as though the conversation closed.

What did he mean? The fear that had snaked around my middle earlier eased a little. Only a little. He pulled a book from his pocket and I gazed from the window as London passed by in a dripping blur.

I had met him but thrice before our marriage.

Six months ago, my brothers arranged a business dinner. Our humble townhouse had been scrubbed top to bottom. A chore I'd learned to do when our household had been reduced to one maid and a cook. That day, the maid quit for better pay, leaving me alone to do the serving. I remember donning the starched apron with some satisfaction. Home-keeping had come naturally to me. I enjoyed it for the most part.

I'd been summoned to the parlor and officially introduced. He bowed, I curtsied. The remainder of the evening, I appeared as an invisible maid, having changed my clothes and pinned the curls back from my face. I imagined he never guessed who wore the mop cap and apron.

The second time was in Carl and Trevor's office at the shipyard. I'd been delivering luncheon. My brothers were absent but he, Lord Sherborne, was there waiting. He turned at my entry.

"Good day, my lord."

"Miss Dawes."

"Please excuse me."

He bowed. I curtsied. No spark of interest flickered.

He then appeared at the funerals for Trevor and Matthew. Naught else between us but a marriage proposal, a wedding, and a long stretch of road...

Hours later, I jolted awake. Arms were about me, the scent of balsam invaded my senses as a cold mist wet my face. A lantern glowed, a door creaked open. Before I could think straight, Lord Sherborne set me on my feet. "Can you walk?"

I nodded, exhaustion flooding my being. I wearily looked about a well-kept inn, though little I could see by candlelight. Two maids appeared at my side. "Right this way, Lady Sherborne."

My new name. No longer would I be called Miss Dawes. Many a day since I'd employed a lady's maid. I followed them up a narrow stair, Lord Sherborne followed.

A footman met us at the top and bowed. "My Lord."

Lord Sherborne nodded then turned to me. "Rest well. We travel early—your maids will see to waking you."

I scarcely remember the next minutes. The maids helped me remove my cloak and gown, untied my corset, and turned down the bed. I crawled beneath the blankets and my toes met blissful warmth.

"Goodnight, Lady Sherborne. Pull the bell if you need us." They curtsied and left me alone to the fresh memory of the day.

Lady Sherborne...the name became the whisper of a frayed memory as I drifted off to sleep. Had I not heard the name before?

Lady Sherborne...

Chapter Two

Hunger squeezed. When had I eaten last? I blinked in the pale morning light remembering the weight of what I'd done the day before. I was a married woman. Lady Sherborne.

One of the maids wheeled a tea cart into my room and pressed a hand to my shoulder to be sure I was awake. "Lord Sherborne desires to be traveling within the hour, my lady. I'll return in fifteen minutes to help you dress."

I pulled the blankets down and shivered. No time to wait for the maid to build a fire in the grate. My only recourse was the teapot. I slipped from the bed and pressed the warm belly of the brown clay pot between my hands. "For this grace, Lord, I thank thee…" I closed my eyes and prayed for the family I'd left behind.

I swallowed a cup of tea and managed to eat the plate of eggs and ham. My body ached from the hours in the coach the day before. How many more until we reached Lord Sherborne's estate? And why his press to return? His urgency nagged.

A little more time to grow accustomed to the idea of marriage to this stranger seemed ideal, but perhaps would have merely prolonged the pain of knowing what I had to do, and not yet having done it.

A knock sounded and the maid entered. She helped me dress in one of my older gowns, assuredly warmer than the one I spoke my vows in. Did she wonder at my patched clothing?

When I was dressed, Lord Sherborne was already at the coach waiting for me.

A muscle twitched in his cheek. Concern lined his forehead. For me? Handsome, to be sure. Darkly so. At first glance, one might wonder if there was goodness in him. A horse stamped its hoof. Someone swore in the distance, but Sherborne's voice covered the offensive language. "Good morning. I trust you slept well?"

He handed me into the coach.

"I don't remember much." Our few hours of rest failed to abate my exhaustion. Little did I desire to rock about on the road for another day. Or two?

He nodded. "You were that tired?"

I had not been able to sleep the night before. The coach door closed behind us and we were once again quiet strangers.

A large basket sat upon the floor. "There is no tavern between here and Goodwyn Abbey."

"Goodwyn Abbey?"

"Home."

The word carried much meaning. My family had left the only home I'd ever known—and the gracious society to which it belonged, and moved to the townhouse. A much smaller accommodation—a respectable distance from the docks. But never was it home...How could it be without Mother and Father present?

Aunt Honora did her best, but she had been accustomed to a higher mode of living. Trimming our purchases down to the very basics and serving us a regular diet of fish and only an occasional taste of ham had made for a more comfortable corset, but Aunt Honora remained scandalized by our lack. She had once been a beauty among society's drawing rooms. *If we could only purchase beef*—her regular complaint. I wish she'd been able to come with me, but dear Lyvia needed help with the children.

I'd never been more than thirty miles from London—and certainly never in this direction. The carriage jerked forward and I realized that I hadn't asked where we were going. I only knew that it was far from home. The words of Aunt Honora and Carl had blended together like many foreboding musical notes. Ominous warnings about what would happen if I did not agree to this marriage. I heard nothing else, thought nothing else. Asked nothing else. Our ship was sinking and only I could save what little remained of our dignity.

Had grief so stunted my ability to think clearly beyond this one matter? Yet, the offer of marriage had been made but three days ago. I'd little time to prepare. I cleared my throat. "Pardon me."

"Yes?"

"I do not know where we are or where we go." The confession embarrassed.

His brows lifted in surprise. "Do you not? Your brother did not see fit to tell you?"

I answered with a question. "Where is Goodwyn Abbey?"

"Staffordshire." He said with a nod.

My breath left me. "So far."

"From London, yes."

"How often do you travel to Town?"

He removed his hat and ran a hand through his tousled hair. "Last year I traveled four times."

So there was hope I might see my family again. But he quickly dashed the thought away.

"I do not plan to go back any time soon."

Did he not have a seat in the House of Lords? "I had hoped to return..." I swallowed. Would he think me impertinent? "To see my family. Sometime in the future."

He observed me, those pale blue eyes of his always assessing what he saw. "I should not think you would want to see them again. Not after..." His eyes briefly roved to the window. "Everything."

What could he mean? "Not after what?" Why wouldn't I want to see my beloved family?

His mouth drew a grave line. "You do not know." He made a statement, yet it bulged with a question.

"Tell me." I wouldn't rest until I understood what he meant by those terrible words.

He was quiet for a moment, then nodded. "It is only fair that you should know. Your brother contacted some of his old friends...a note went around." He pressed his hands against his knees and leaned forward. "He purposed to sell you to the highest bidder."

Carl? Sell me? What on earth did Lord Sherborne mean? "I don't believe it." Sisters couldn't be sold, could they?

Lord Sherborne blanched at my rejection. "I didn't want to believe it either." He pulled a folded sheet of paper from his pocket. "I intercepted his plan."

He held the incriminating words out to me and I read them. Carl's handwriting, clear and calculating, had thought of everything to save his family from ruin. Including sacrificing his own sister. The inconceivable situation strangled me. My breath shallowed. "You were the highest bidder, I take it."

"No—" His rejection of my judgment sliced the air. "You wouldn't have been necessarily *wed* to one of his friends."

I mentally counted the gentleman of his acquaintance. Most of them were married. "Then..." The truth sickened me.

"If it makes you feel better, your Aunt was against his plan."

She knew? "I would never have followed through with such—" I waved my hand to fill in the sentence I couldn't utter.

He tossed out names with a sneer on his lips. "Lord Gerton. Lord Fendwick. Sir Heeton..."

The faces of widowed, aging gentlemen rose to surface. Carl would have pressured me into marriage with one of them? Surely there could have been another way.

"So instead of marrying an ancient peer, I am now bonded to a perfect stranger." A cry formed in my throat. I wouldn't let it out. Couldn't.

Concern pinched between his eyes and urgency laced his tone. "My apologies. It was the only way I could protect you."

Protect me from the same destitution that would smother my family? Is that what he meant? Marriage to an old man might have been less dangerous than to this stranger. I did not know. "That Carl would have taken my fate into his hands like this..." It didn't make sense. We'd always been a tight-knit family. I'd been closer to Trevor, however. But now Trevor was gone. Forever.

Lord Sherborne shook his head. "If I had not—*blast*."

"Do you regret our union?" My words dangled. I wished I hadn't spoken.

He jerked to face me and took one of my hands. His mouth parted and lines deepened across his forehead. The air pulsed between us as though we were both on the edge of a cliff and I was about to fall a great distance. His hold tightened. "It was the only way."

Hope fled. He released my hand as fear crept along my shoulders and replaced the small amount of peace I'd gained. I was certain from that moment forward, that Lord Sherborne did indeed have regrets. And I was the culmination of them. A choice forced upon him.

I looked back down at Carl's writing. There my name stained the paper in inky dark letters, *Miss Elaina Dawes, a virtuous woman, available for any man's pleasure.* Marriage hadn't been a requirement. My stomach soured at Carl's intentions. My face flashed with heat as I remembered his pleading my marriage to Lord Sherborne. *"If you don't wed him, you will cause my children to starve."*

If Lord Sherborne hadn't intercepted Carl's plan, I could not fathom the burden he would have placed upon me. As though I was the guilty party. Who had truly been at fault for the Dawes Shipping's failure? Did not Carl and Trevor hold the reins? Being a gentleman's daughter, I'd offered to serve as a governess and send money home. But Carl had tossed the idea as hopeless. The few coins I'd receive would hardly be helpful.

Caroline had abandoned us. Father, Mother, Trevor, and Matthew gone. Must more shadow be cast upon the Dawes? How could further sins be atoned for? My life lived as Carl planned wouldn't do it.

Carl hadn't embraced me in our grief. He'd shifted beneath a hard shell while the rest of us wept openly. I crinkled the edges of this abomination—this advertisement for...me. Was this why he avoided me? Because he was going to sacrifice me?

I took in the words once again as hurt and fury fought a strange duel. He would have betrayed me to a half-life. My own brother.

A large pair of hands pulled at the letter. "I should never have shown you. Let it go, Elaina." His deep voice softened as tears slipped from my eyes. He used my given name.

I willed my vise grip on the paper to weaken as he slid it from my hands. "You were right to tell me," I whispered. "Thank you."

He folded the letter and put it back in his coat pocket. "I am sorry. Family should always behave as such. No one should ever be treated as chattle. Ever." The blue eyes I had thought cold turned compassionate.

Tears fell. I'd been on the brink of drowning within Carl's betrayal. I might still.

Lord Sherborne slipped to my side of the coach, an arm about my shoulders. A handkerchief presented itself, his warm dry cloak a refuge for my grief. This stranger, why did he help me? Why did he help Carl at all? His claim of guilt made no sense. The Zephyr hit the rocks, her men and goods dispersed.

I too am at sea.

Sinking.

A few hours later, still drowsy I pulled away from his side, salty tears marring my complexion. He eased his arm away and took his seat across from me.

"You are too kind." I did all I could to compose myself.

"Had I been kinder sooner." No further words were needed.

I suddenly felt on the winning side of a harsh, unknown game my brother had been playing. What else did he think to do? I questioned ever truly having known him but my thoughts also transitioned into something more significant.

Carl was not the ship's captain, nor the sailor, nor the smugglers that had lured them to perceived safety. He'd not sunk the Zephyr. Nor had Lord Sherborne. Someone had predicted its demise, he'd said. But no one could do that. Aside from the wicked stranger who'd lifted a lantern high as to deceive safe harbor, the ship's fate had been out of everyone's hands. So that left me with a fact I couldn't conceive. If Carl had been willing to do this evil against me, what had he already done? Desperate men do desperate things—the cliché bounded about my mind.

Lyvia couldn't have known what he'd planned. She would have warned me, surely. Or would she have? Why hadn't Aunt Honora done the right thing?

Lord Sherborne lifted the basket from the floor. "You must be hungry."

How did one go on eating and breathing after discovering a beloved brother's duplicity? Death would have been easier to bear. Aunt Honora suggested I'd been born to save the family. Even for someone as vile as my brother? What a twisted proposition.

I took an offered chunk of bread and cheese and looked at my husband. I wondered how life could change with the strike of a flint, the glow of a lantern, and the desperate plans of men.

Lord Sherborne chewed his food, then paused. "We are not the strangers you believe us to be."

Chapter Three

"At least not the perfect stranger you insinuate." He waited for a response.

"Are we not?"

"No, Lady Sherborne." His lips curved in a tender smile.

The name—it woke in me again a familiarity that memory could not touch. "I enjoyed only a single London Season, four years ago now."

He tipped his chin. "You had so many suitors, I couldn't get near."

He tried to know me then? The burn of a blush crept along my collar. He was right. I did have many suitors. But surely, I would have remembered the tall baron edging his way around the crowds. Balls and parties were designed for such fortuitous matches—especially for my ilk.

At the time, I was rather taken with Sir William de Fort. Dashing, energetic. Altogether the wrong sort, I later discovered. While I was a gentleman's daughter, my pick had been among sons of knights and baronets. No hope for the lofty title I now bore.

He shrugged. "It's true."

"Did we meet?"

"We did."

"Where?"

"At the opera."

The opera...I shook my head, embarrassed. "As you said, I had many suitors." The season had been utterly distracting and had failed miserably when Caroline eloped. The suitors fled as the whisper of scandal tainted my potential for a good match. My dowry had not been large enough to tempt anyone to withstand the Ton's judgments.

"You trounced upon my foot and gave an apology." He smiled for the first time. "My father introduced us."

That meant—his father knew mine? For no other reason were introductions made. "I vaguely remember stumbling over someone."

"I do not wonder that you don't remember. Your family has endured much since then." He brushed crumbs from his coat and finished his bread in silence.

We'd arrive at Goodwyn Abbey this night. What would his parents think of his choice of bride? And then it struck me. Lord Sherborne had inherited much. His own father was deceased.

"Has your mother been apprised of our marriage?" Her shock might well surpass mine.

His eyes grew distant and uncomfortable. "She has been gone these three years."

"I am sorry." I glanced through the window. Still and all, there'd be no mother-in-law to appease. Dark clouds gathered once again. Rain pelted the roof of the coach with such strength, it drowned out any attempt to speak.

In truth, I needed to gather my own thoughts, but like the rain, they splashed into a murky muddle. My saving was to be the mistress of Goodwyn Abbey. A new life. A wife to one who paid my family's debts and rescued me from nefarious plans.

I'd often thought about my chances for success with love and marriage. Had blamed Caroline more times than I could count for my lack of it. But what was love, really? Those fleeing suitors hadn't the capacity for love or they wouldn't have abandoned me. Or pretended interest and flirted with me in order to climb a little higher up the societal ladder. A shameful way to gain a wife – or treat a tender heart.

Lord Sherborne paid the price of regret—was the only way to keep me safe, he'd said. I touched the ring he'd placed upon my finger. A pence for a promise, a promise for a pence. He'd nothing to gain by his association with me. Nothing at all.

How gallant of him to make me think he'd wanted to know me those years ago. But that was impossible. A man of his consequence required a woman of greater rank. In retrospect, I'm fairly certain that had my parents noticed his interest—and banked on their acquaintance with him—the waters would have miraculously parted and a hasty courtship would have ensued.

Through half-shuddered eyes, he observed my interest in the ring he'd bestowed my hand. A day's growth peppered his jaws.

"It is a beautiful ring." I whispered. A choking swell of grief caught within my throat as the present collided with the past.

"It looks well on your hand."

I squirmed under his regard. My hands had grown less soft these past four years. "Have you no siblings?" I asked.

He shook his head. Then we would be quite alone. With no betraying brothers and no unsuspecting sisters.

Night had fallen by the time we reached Goodwyn Abbey. The stone edifice rose as high as London's church spires in dark, shadowed points. Entry lanterns glowed, revealing high cathedral arches over the doorway. What lay behind these walls?

We exited the coach and climbed the few steps and through the ancient set of doors that opened to pools of glowing candles. The butler, housekeeper, and a smattering of sleepy-eyed servants lined the hall.

Lord Sherborne bent to my ear. "I sent word ahead of our arrival."

They bowed and curtsied as we passed.

"Mrs. Chambers. We will take supper in our rooms."

"Yes, my lord." The aged housekeeper eyed me and smiled.

Hands tugged and pulled my cloak away from my body and I shivered. The air had grown cooler.

"Build up the fire for Lady Sherborne, Nancy." He offered me his arm. "I will take you up."

We climbed a red carpeted flagstone stair that curved sharply to one side. Tapestries covered the walls in scenes of an ancient past. A sword glinted in the candlelight, along with a shield that boasted a fierce griffin.

Down the wide hall, a door hung open. More light flickered within. He ushered me through and I was surprised to see a large parlor of sorts. A fire snapped in the fireplace and candles burned bright to reveal a comfortable looking davenport, and a small dining table set for two. A desk sat in one corner below a window—and a shelf of books.

"I daresay you don't want to sit down just yet." He smiled.

He was right. I didn't. The fire drew me. I'd been cold for days, except for the delirious warmth of my bed last night.

He pointed to a door situated on the right. "Your rooms are through there." He pointed again to the door on our left. "That leads to my quarters."

I nodded. I wasn't sure what to expect of our sudden marriage. The strangeness of its reason, my transportation from a small London townhouse to this vast place, clouded my thinking.

Servants carried food to the table and shut the door behind them. My appetite had waned after the day's revelations. But when Lord Sherborne took the lid away from the soup tureen, my mouth watered. Hot stew and fresh bread. Sustenance of the best kind. *Lord, for this grace, I thank thee...*

"Elaina."

I looked up from my plate. "Lord Sherborne?"

"My name is Zander. You may use it. Please?"

I nodded. "Zander. Yes, my lord."

"You aren't a servant, Elaina. Just Zander. I am not your lordship."

I set down my fork, realizing my mistake. I had much to relearn if I were going to be a proper baron's wife. I'd quite given up on the social graces that Aunt Honora required.

"Things will seem better in the morning," he said. "And one day, you will wake up to find this mess far behind you."

This mess. The tangled painful mess the Dawes brothers no doubt created. One that snagged a baron for a benefactor. I wasn't sure I could be extricated from the aching humiliation. What possible value would I bring to one such as he?

He rose from his chair. "Rest well, we will meet in the morning and I will give you a tour. Introduce you to the staff. Nancy will be waiting for you in your rooms." He bowed and left me sitting before a crust of bread I was too tired to chew.

Lord Sherborne...Zander...my husband. What business had he with the Dawes brothers aside from investments? How much had he lost when the Zephyr sank?

I stepped into my rooms and sat before the vanity mirror while Nancy brushed the knots from my hair. I was poor company, to be sure.

Soon, I snuggled beneath the blankets in a grand bed draped with heavy green curtains. The fire had been allowed to blaze high per Lord Sherborne's instructions. He knew I'd appreciate the warmth. His thoughtfulness bode well.

How is it that the kindness of a stranger is more than a brother's? Tears smarted once again. The brother I once knew had died. Both were now lost. I wept.

Should I be angry with Aunt Honora? Had she only meant to spare me the worst? Should I confront her about the matter? The night dragged slowly and the fire died down. I lay awake weeping and listening to the creaks and groans of this strange abbey. My new home.

Chapter Four

I slept the remainder of the night without moving. I'd woken to someone speaking, not quietly. "No, my lord, she still sleeps." A maid.

I blinked awake to the sun blazing as it hadn't for days, but the chill in the air still snapped. I rolled over to see the fire had been built up. For me. The hearth was no longer filled with the lifeless ash that seemed to fuel my despair. If the sun could rise despite what happened beneath it, so could I.

A throat cleared. "My lady, you're awake." The maid curtsied. "I'll return with your breakfast." She opened her hand toward the door I'd entered. "Lord Sherborne would speak with you when you are ready."

Another maid replaced her. She quickly helped me dress—my trunks had been delivered sometime during last night's supper. Strange to see mementos of my old home in this new one. But not unwelcome.

"Thank you, Nancy." I caught my reflection in the mirror as she arranged my hair. Dark circles stained beneath red-rimmed eyes. Exhaustion pulled them taut.

Breakfast boasted a generous porridge bowl along with poached eggs and toast. I would not go hungry here. The tea was hot and strong and completely fortifying.

But I rushed the meal to join Lord Sherborne—Zander. Mustn't keep him waiting. An estate as vast as this one surely required a great deal of time. That and whatever it was that drove him to return so quickly.

With a turn of the knob, I entered our shared living space. He sat at the desk scribbling away but rose from his chair at my arrival. He set a piece of stationary over his writing. Why? So that I wouldn't see, perhaps?

"Elaina." He crossed the room to where I stood. "You've been weeping." He cupped my face with his hands, gently brushing his thumbs at the bruises beneath my eyes. I warmed at his familiarity—the concern reflected in his eyes owned a mysterious depth. He cared but I didn't understand why. "I am so very sorry." He dropped his hands as I began to ease. "You've much to grieve."

Much, yes.

He turned and walked to the window—waved me to join him. "Our parlor looks out upon the gardens."

I joined him and looked down. Were we so high? I didn't remember climbing so many steps last night.

"Took a few years to set it right again. One would never know that it was abandoned and left to grow wild."

Below me was a maze—where one might meander and not be seen for a time. To the right and left of it grew rose vines, recently devoid of blooms. Tall trees bent around the garden in perfect order, except for two that were set back and permitted to grow at will. Branches dipped and poked the sky. T'would be beautiful come spring. If only a quiet turn about those paths might lead to quieter thoughts and a healed heart.

Wind picked up a swirl of leaves along the walkway and rattled them off the trees. A dog bounded among them. Did he belong to Zander? Surely he wouldn't permit a feral beast to roam.

"I must warn you, don't go into the maze until I can show you how to exit."

"I feel as though lost in the midst of one now." Long and snaking with no end in sight.

"I am here, Elaina." A tender smile.

He meant to reassure me that I wasn't lost. Would he truly guide me out of grief and betrayal? "Yes—but—who are you?" I asked the question—one among many. I pressed a hand between my eyes. "Forgive me. I assume our acquaintance will take time." As kind as he'd been, I still didn't know if I could trust him. Once upon a time, I assumed my brother to also be a good man.

He seemed momentarily at a loss at my query. He gathered my hand that bore his ring into his own. "One that promises to care for you as no brother could. I must ask you to trust me." His dark brows willed me to accept his plea. He understood what I meant to say.

Blind trust was a frightening proposition. I had no other choice. My hand hovered between us, clasped in his strength. A flash of warmth enveloped me. The gentlemanly hold he had on my hand, the heat from his fingers spread to mine. "I didn't mean to sound so..."

I allowed my gaze to take in his features. From the clean-shaven jaw to the set of his eyes. His facial features gave way to a handsome chin. No, I am certain I would have remembered him. Too remarkable a bearing to forget. Perhaps he was right. Much had happened since the night at the opera.

At that moment I did indeed remember. Only it wasn't the opera where I'd trounced his foot. It was the theater. I gasped at the recollection, as it flew to the surface of my memories.

"What is it?" Concern filled his eyes again. I was quite the menagerie of emotions. How often Aunt Honora begged me to stop wearing them on my sleeve. What choice did I have? They wouldn't fit in my pocket.

"I remembered the first time we met." I shook my head. "How strange that I couldn't before." It was the night Caroline had eloped. "I..." More like returned. "You helped us to our carriage after...Mother was beside herself..."

"Yes."

The cruel cut had begun that very night. Gossip had spread like fire, Mother wept openly. We had to navigate a path through the frowning, judging crowds, the many turned backs.

Father had Mother by the elbow and I trailed behind as fast as I could. That's when I'd tripped. A strong arm caught me. This man's. He led me to the carriage with a whisper. "Hold your head high, Miss Dawes..." And then, we raced away and I hadn't seen him again until last year—only I hadn't recognized him. So closed I've been to recollections of that time! It had been a night so horrible I'd refused to entertain a thought of it, let alone a memory.

Why had my situation mattered to him even then? Questions bloomed one after another.

"Here," he offered his arm. "You should know your way about Goodwyn. I'll show you around."

We exited the parlor door and made our way back down the staircase. As formidable as it had appeared in the darkness, the daylight revealed its strong bones. Arches met arches like jangled ribcages joining and separating as rooms had been divided up for other uses. Stained glass windows bled a rainbow of colors upon the stone walls. The rainbow, a sacred promise that the earth wouldn't be again drowned beneath water. I blinked at the irony. My entire world now rested beneath the waves.

Zander led me into a bright receiving room of faded blues and greens, where I'd greet guests and neighbors who happened to call. A pretty place that seemed altogether abandoned. Then the library—full of leather and musty air, enough books to last a lifetime. My life may be lonely here, except for these teeming shelves.

The medieval dining hall looked as though it hadn't changed in centuries. Jacobean furniture filled the room, thick and ornately carved, it would have overpowered our simple dining space at home. Its long age-darkened table and high chairs numbered more than thirty. And I was to be mistress of all of this? It hardly seemed real.

"Do you entertain much?"

"Nay. We host but three dinners every year—last year perhaps only one."

The dinners I'd once enjoyed were social events that pitted one rank over another, amid flirtations and plans devised by mothers and fathers alike to build more wealth among the already rich. To tempt, if without monetary resources. Entrapments that drew pompous young men away from financial equals—or offered opportunities for titled gentlemen and women to restock their coffers.

Being so long away from such affairs gave me a view into what I'd left behind. In the thick of it, my head had been filled with the haze and dazzle of a mere mimicry of love and friendship. Once I'd seen the truth of it, I did not care to return to the lie. I'd be expected to hostess dinners, but Zander didn't seem the sort of man that played at society life. Or did he?

Another mystery poked about my mind. I'd caught glimpses of genuine friendships, laughter, and joy—all behind the glow of the cottage windows along my street. But I'd never experienced this type of gathering, outside of the kind old vicar at home who would stay for tea and answer any questions I plied him with. The expectation weighed. I knew how to host, but I would never again be what I was. Unless Zander might expect it? Would he?

I followed him through the door, and into a dark corridor. The ceiling shrank above us until an inch above his head.

"My study is here." Zander pulled open a low door. "Where I do most of my work when I'm not out amongst our tenants."

"Tenants?" I hadn't thought of it, but of course. Nearly every estate had them.

"Some twenty families depend upon Goodwyn land."

My heart warmed at the thought that this place wasn't so desolate. People lived here—and thrived, I hoped. I glanced around. Two large leather chairs poised before a fireplace, a thick fur rug between them. A wide, heavily carved desk sat along the opposite wall, completely cluttered with papers. Shelves of ledgers, the scent of ash and wax.

"If you ever need me, chances are, I'll be here."

I nodded, somehow comforted.

He led me back through the low corridor and up the stairs—down the opposite hall from our rooms. Here, family portraits lined the path, far from the doings of the household. Men and women with their own place in history. Odd clothing, wide collars, lace ones. I stifled a laugh, turned, and my breath caught. Here was someone I recognized. Someone I knew by sight. Lady Sherborne.

"My mother."

I was never acquainted with her, but well I knew her visage and name. Much admired about Town. "She was very beautiful." Another thread of memory yet pulled.

He turned to me with questioning brows. Did he expect me to think or say otherwise? He pointed to another painting of a man much like the one who stood beside me. "My father."

The only other Sherborne I'd met—one who well knew my father. An investor in Dawes Shipping, no doubt. The Dawes company had many investors, all of whom lost everything when the Zephyr sank. Perhaps I need not be concerned with my new position in society, that honor lay at the bottom of the ocean regardless that marriage had changed my name.

"Some unused bed chambers are through there." He pointed down a corridor I hadn't seen. By some trick of low lighting, I had assumed the wall ended where the portraits stopped. "We haven't hosted guests for many years. No doubt the rooms moulder." He shrugged. "I won't waste our time by bothering the housekeeper for the keys."

I peered down the dark hall, lit only by a few small windows. Cobwebs filled the corners of the doorways. "Another day, perhaps."

I followed his lead back to our common sitting room where a maid had delivered tea. She poured our cups and left us alone. I swallowed the hot liquid yet nothing seemed to chase the chill.

A knock sounded at the door and a middle-aged man entered, a woman close on his heels. "Good morning, my lord. My lady." A swift nod in my direction.

Zander set his teacup down. "Lady Sherborne, this is my secretary, Mr. Thomhow, and his wife, Mrs. Thomhow."

Mrs. Thomhow curtsied. "About time Goodwyn Abbey had a mistress again." Her smile shone like the bright red curls piled atop her head. "It's been far too long."

"A pleasure to make your acquaintance." At least I certainly hoped so.

Mr. Thomhow bore a bulging leather satchel. "The pleasure is all ours, Lady Sherborne." His smile changed from polite to solemn as he slipped a letter from the satchel and handed it to Zander.

He stiffened.

Mr. Thomhow responded to the question that Zander seemed to be asking. "It is, my lord."

He opened the missive and took it to the window to read. His jaw grew taut as he scanned the words. "When did it come?"

"This morning, not but a half hour since."

He nodded. "We've no time to lose."

"I'll send for your man." Mr. Thomhow exited the room.

"Mrs. Thomhow, see that my wife has every provision." Zander turned to me. "Forgive me—I'll have to show you the grounds another day." He glanced quickly at the door. "I've received word that—I must go." He bowed and left.

"Come, Lady Sherborne." Mrs. Thomhow poured a cup of tea, her smile undimmed by the odd message and departure of the men. "Let us become acquainted then, shall we?"

Chapter Five

Mrs. Thomhow didn't know how I came to be mistress of Goodwyn Hall, that much I gathered. But neither did she pry. If her questioning eyes could dig and reveal the facts, she would, no doubt, be scandalized.

I wouldn't have minded telling her the whole truth, but I didn't know if I should. Or if Zander would desire it to be never more discussed, and certainly not with household staff. I kept the conversation going by asking her everything I could about the abbey, the grounds, and its tenants. And the village. She was more than happy to oblige. As a resident of the place, she'd been a companion to the former Lady Sherborne for a year before her death. However I have yet to discover the true nature of her employment since, other than being the wife of Zander's secretary. Was she expected to be my companion also?

Though pleasant, I grew very tired. Luncheon was brought in for the two of us during which I had to hide more than a few yawns behind my napkin. The grievous night pressed upon me and my eyelids grew heavy.

"Forgive me, you are fatigued." She stood from the table. "No one would blame you after the long journey you've had. There now." She set her napkin on the table. "Go take a rest."

"You are right. I'm about to fall asleep over pudding." How embarrassing that would be.

She gave my shoulder a friendly touch and left the room. The silence enveloped me and I felt I could sleep where I stood. But a flash of something white jolted me awake. There, by the corner of the tea table, was the missive that made Zander leave so quickly. Finally, a chance to learn something for myself.

I scurried to the message before a servant could come and clear away the dishes and tucked it into my pocket as Nancy walked in a split second later.

It was for him really. No need for the wrong eyes to see what didn't belong to them. Whatever was in this note was Zander's business. But was it also mine? A tendril of guilt flared, but I tamped it down.

"I will lie down and would like to be left undisturbed for a few hours."

"Yes, m'lady." She curtsied. "I will build up the fire before I take these downstairs."

"Thank you."

"M'lady." Another curtsy.

Exhaustion tugged, the message burned. Was most likely some business details I wouldn't understand or care a whit about. I stepped into my room as Nancy left and climbed upon my bed. I waited until I could no longer hear the clink of dishes and retreating footsteps to read what Zander had dropped in haste.

A knock sounded and I shoved the paper beneath my dress. Mrs. Thomhow entered. "You have everything you need, my dear?" My heart pounded for nothing. Why need I hide the letter? And why had she returned after just parting?

"Indeed I do."

She nodded and left me again. I took a deep breath and pulled it out.

Dear Sir,

Your inquiry and suspicion has proven correct. You know where to come for further contact. I strongly recommend swift removal.

Yours Respectfully,

Kent Hedge, Esq.

I had been swiftly removed...is that what he meant? But why then, would Lord Sherborne need to hasten? No, he meant something else. Someone else. And what, I wonder, had proven correct? Evidently, Lord Sherborne knew exactly what it meant and where to go.

I hated this small mystery. This knowledge gap. The shock of Carl's betrayal had left a hole in my spirit—how unaware I'd been. How gullible to men's unseen plans. I'd so little time to make sense of everything and my new husband had left me here to fend for myself.

"It was the only way to protect you..." That's what he'd said.

I tucked the message within my bodice and slid beneath the blankets as the heaviness of sleep drew me in. I'd return it to him—I could sneak it into his room and leave it where he'd find it.

I awoke to thunderstorms. Alone. I pulled myself from slumber to see that night had fallen and with it, torrents of rain. I drew back the curtain from the window as lightning struck across the sky. Where had he gone? Was he safe?

Questions I couldn't answer. Had I missed supper? Hunger gnawed. Perhaps I should pull the bell.

I wandered into the parlor where candles had been lit and a fire glowed. A maid walked in carrying a silver platter with a message. Mrs. Thomhow's regrets that she could not join me for supper as her children had become ill. Of course, she ought to stay with them. How many did she have? I thought of my nieces and nephews and the joy they'd brought to me these past difficult years. Never before had I felt such loneliness.

I admit, I needed this stretch of quiet to think about all that had happened and how I might piece my life back together again. What it might look like and how I might fill my days. As it stood, I could barely see a step before me. The future, a thick fog.

I tried to read a book but found myself unable to entertain a story. So distracted was I by these new circumstances. A supper of hot creamy soup, cold chicken, bread, cheese, and fruit arrived by tray and the quiet, the blessed quiet, was a balm to my soul. I dined before the snapping fire and somehow didn't feel as lonely. The flames moved, sparked, and heated as though a living presence sought to ease my hurting heart open, to acknowledge what it hadn't before.

I would have time to be better acquainted with my husband. And mayhap, love him too. The idea burned. That I might come to love my husband... Would he love me in return? Was it possible when such a tragic situation necessitated our very marriage?

I could trust him with my rescue, evidently, and my safety. Could I trust him with my heart? I slipped to the ground in front of the flames and held out my hands. Hearts weren't free for the taking, but they were free for the giving. Why did it feel dangerous to allow myself to long for his return?

Two more days passed in solitude. I had now slept sufficiently to recover from the long carriage ride.

I'd wandered about Goodwyn Abbey for exercise, but didn't venture out of doors. I don't know why—but without Lord Sherborne, I was adrift in this expansive place. I missed him. Exploring without a guide seemed a risk. Never mind that I'd traversed to the London docks and back to our townhome on a regular basis. I knew a few folks along the way—where I might take shelter if ever I was wary of being followed. Shops where I might linger for a few minutes.

It seemed that even here, such wariness might be endured, for everywhere I went, footsteps followed me. Creaks and doors closing where there shouldn't be any such noise. At first, I thought it to be the staff who bustled about the place with their many duties. That was it. Had to be. Sounds might carry along the ancient bones of this massive construction.

I knew no one here, besides Mrs. Thomhow, who no doubt continued to nurse her children. I sent a kind inquiry but had heard nothing back. Family sickness was worrisome. I prayed for her, what else could I do? Perhaps when the danger passed, I might give her some relief and read to the children.

That first morning, I slipped into Lord Sherborne's bedchamber, feeling as though I were trespassing. Furnished in warm browns and greens, the place looked well used, though in perfect order. I slipped the letter from my bodice and quickly placed it within the drawer of a desk. Should I draw his attention to it when he returned? Certainly not. Else he would know that I entered his... a noise shuffled in the hallway and I stilled.

I shut my eyes and willed whoever it was to be gone. Feet pattered away and I took a breath. I escaped back into the parlor with a ridiculous stifled laugh. A wife may sometimes be found in her husband's chamber. There was no wrong in that. I need not be embarrassed before the staff. Yet...

I left the rooms and found my way to the kitchen where the cook and scullery maids stopped in their tracks at my entrance before rushing to see what I needed. Such a cheery place of warmth, industry, and provision! Copper pots gleamed, a spicy scent boiled on the stove, while I was certain that bread baked in the oven. My hands itched to do something, to help. But it was clear that Lady Sherborne's presence made them uncomfortable. I needed to find my place.

If they noticed the roughness of my hands they would understand that I was not a stranger to work. I'd left them but was followed out by the cook. I would need to provide her with a weekly menu soon, if I preferred it. I complimented her cooking, she curtsied and blushed.

And so, once again, I'd been left alone. My imagination churning. Darkness had long since fallen and I paced my bedroom floor unable to sleep. How long would I be left to myself?

Somewhere, a clock struck midnight. Enough. I could not keep to these confining rooms. I donned a robe and meandered downstairs by the glow of my chamberstick. Perhaps the library held an interesting novel to while away these bleak, empty hours.

I found my way easily enough. Clearly the staff had retreated to bed hours ago. I perused the shelves as well as I could with a single flame to guide me. Many classics, poets, and...I was reaching for a book when I heard the crunch of hooves in the distance.

The sound grew nearer. Did Lord Sherborne return? In my haste to watch from the window, the candle flame went out and left me in the darkness with nothing but a half-moon to offer any substitution. I pressed my forehead against the cold glass. There. It was a carriage—the same I'd traveled in—coming down the path. He had returned. My heart beat stronger.

A rustle of movement scampered past the door. I did not relish being caught in my night things without a light and lurking in the shadows. I covered myself with the drapery while still affording a view of the outside. I'd head back to bed as soon as soon as I was certain that my pathway was clear.

The carriage stopped—a servant and stable hand rushed over. Mr. Thomhow exited first, followed by the tall figure of my husband. He lifted something from the coach—a burden of some sort. Zander turned and something slipped from his hold. An arm dangled from the covering.

I pressed my hands against my mouth and stifled a scream. He carried a corpse.

Alarm flooded my being. I dropped to the floor as they faced the front of the house and entered with muffled sounds. A great effort was made to be very quiet. Was this murder? Had the stranger I married became a fearsome thing? What had he been doing and why bring death to this house?

The message mentioned swift removal. Could be, whoever it was, had died and somehow demanded Lord Sherborne's tending. Need I think of murder? Perhaps all would come clear on the morrow. The deceased would be buried, and I would learn of a poor tenant's unfortunate demise. Like those who lurked around the docks, who spent their lives drinking and gambling away the sober moments. Perhaps this place was no different. Zander appeared to be the kind of man who rescued the needy, rather than the opposite. Only for that poor fellow, it was far too late.

I blew out a breath of calming air. Indeed, I had no reason to think Zander a criminal. I reprimanded myself. My imagination had run away with me in this old, creaky place.

Sounds grew distant but I remained where I was. Soon, I'd be safe enough to go back upstairs. I know not how long I waited. I dozed off in a dream of a carriage ride that never ended, a fate never found. I jolted awake in the dead silence of the library. The floor had grown colder than before and my body felt stiff and sore. I peeked out of the window, still dark but maybe not for long. I must hasten to my room before anything was found to be amiss.

How would it seem that the new lady of the house wandered about like a sleepwalker? I grimaced at the thought and snatched a book – any book – from the shelf. It was, after all, what I'd been after in the first place.

I opened the library door and peered down the hall. Weak light graced the stairway. In less than a minute, I'd be in my own warm bed. I dashed for the steps but ran into a rock-hard table—pain plunged into my stomach as I doubled over, gasping. I stumbled backward into something.

I turned, and there before me was a towering giant. He shouted with large, mishappen teeth in a snarl, grabbed me by the shoulders and shook. Hard. A scream tore through my throat and blackness swallowed me.

Chapter Six

Something pungent filled my nostrils and a vise held my wrist as I jerked to the present.

"Calm you down, lass. I'm only trying to help."

I blinked to see a white-haired, bespectacled man beside me with a pocket watch next to his ear and a firm thumb taking my pulse.

He released my wrist. "Sounds good enough."

Light streamed in the room, but was so dull I couldn't decipher the time of day. I blinked and turned my head. Lord Sherborne stood at the end of my bed while two maids waited near the door. Why were so many people in my room? I shifted and tried to rise. My stomach hurt—then I remembered. Running into the wide, marble-topped table. The man...and that body...

Zander cleared his throat, "Molly, fetch some tea."

The maid dashed away.

"I don't understand." My voice croaked.

The doctor patted my hand. "Be calm for a moment while I check your abdomen." He looked to Zander. "May I?"

He nodded and shifted his posture to face away from me.

Gentle hands pressed and probed. "I heard you had a run-in with the cloak table." His fingers found a tender place and I sucked in a breath. "While fetching a volume of Greek poetry." He removed his hands and pulled the blanket back up to my chin. "There now. I think no harm done. You will have some bruising and will probably be sore for a short time. I must ask that you stay abed for a few days to be safe."

Zander shook his hand. "Thank you, Doctor Rillian."

"Good day, Lady Sherborne. I'm sorry to have met you under less than pleasant circumstances."

I nodded.

"Good day, Doctor." Zander motioned to Nancy. "You may go."

We were alone.

Zander pulled a chair beside my bed and sat. "I'm afraid my arrival must have disturbed you from sleep." He offered me the book I'd lost when I'd fainted. Black speckles peppered his face—he hadn't shaved in days. His hair of coal black waves tossed about, handsome as always.

I gulped. "I couldn't sleep..." Did he suspect that I saw what he delivered under the cover of night?

Concern lit his eyes. "Does it hurt much?"

I shifted to sit up. "Lord Sherborne..."

One brow rose.

"I mean, Zander."

He smiled, though exhaustion pressed around his eyes. "I'm sorry that I had to rush off like I did. I hear Mrs. Thomhow hasn't been able to attend to you." He took my hand that wore his ring. "I hope you weren't too lonely."

Molly arrived with the tea tray, poured us each a cup, and left. I fingered the fine bone china, white with blue filigree. "I freely admit that I was."

"You spent much time with your brother's children, I think."

"Yes. And Aunt Honora." I took a sip. "Never a dull moment." And the Sunday school children I had the pleasure to teach. I'd wanted to do something for the children of my parish—many of them couldn't read and didn't know that God had made them with a purpose. In London, even away from society of the Ton, I'd made a busy life—both by requirement and ambition.

"You've scarcely a moment to adjust to your new living." He wiped a hand across his eyes. "I am sorry. It couldn't be helped."

I waited for him to tell me the tale of the tenant who'd died. Of the unfortunate soul he'd been burdened with burying. He said nothing. Not one word.

He thumbed through the book I'd snagged from the shelf without thought. "Have I a classically educated wife?"

"Indeed no." What would he think of me? Naught but the expected French and a very little Latin. "My candle went out and..."

"You made a blind grab and hoped for the best?" His lips quirked as though trying to hold back a laugh. "You poor soul. A high price to pay for a book you cannot read." He drummed his fingers on the hardcover. "Perhaps it might be best to arrange a shelf for you here—so that you don't have to go traipsing about this precarious place at ungodly hours."

I felt ridiculous, sitting in my bed in naught but my nightclothes—he beside me. "Of course."

"Tell me your preferences and I'll fetch them for you. Especially since you are bound to this bed for a few days."

I sighed. I'd already felt imprisoned for days on end.

"I don't know how to tell you. Perhaps he is a servant that I haven't met. I don't know. But there was a stranger—a large man. I know I wasn't dreaming. He screamed and shook me—that's all I remember."

Zander's brows rose as he nodded. "Callum. You gave him quite a fright. He's been waiting in the other room. He is rather sorry about all that."

"Callum?"

"My ward."

"How did I not meet him before?"

"Housekeeper says he's been hiding since you arrived." He leaned forward. "Callum is one of God's children. I beg you be patient with him." He set the book aside. "If he doesn't apologize to you soon, he'll be impossible to live with. May I allow him in?"

"Of course."

Zander tenderly kissed my hand. "Thank you." He opened the door and a moment later came back, pulling Callum behind him.

His hulking form took small steps like a child, his head was bent and tears streamed down his dark cheeks. In the other hand, he clutched something that looked like flowers.

"Callum, may I present to you Lady Sherborne." He took the boy's large hand.

Callum shifted close to my side and bowed before crumpling to his knees in penitence. "I hurt y' badly, mum. I didn't mean t' hurt y'." His regret rent my heart. The simple-hearted man offered paper flowers to me with his head still bowed.

I received the newspaper blossoms as from a child. "How beautiful. Thank you." I lay a hand on his massive black mane of hair. "I think I must have frightened you."

He rose. "Thought y' were a ghost cum t' take me to the forest. I don't want to go to the forest." Those mishappen teeth grimaced with fear.

Zander put an arm about his shoulders. "No one will ever make you go to the forest again. Now, let us leave Lady Sherborne to her rest."

"I am pleased to meet you Callum. I hope we can be good friends."

Zander shot me a look of gratitude before guiding him through the door. "No more hiding about, Callum. You've nothing to fear from my wife, I assure you."

A moment later, he returned and poured me another cup of tea. "I should share with you how he came to be here."

I had been wondering.

"Gypsies squatted on the land for several months before traveling to a new place. I was a child. Our gamekeeper found him alone in the woods—abandoned and starving. Naught but four years old. My mother took pity on him. Father thought to return him to his people but knew they would only abandon him again because of his differences. The risk of his death was too great, so my parents chose to protect him. As you see, his is a very fearful soul."

"He appears to be gentle enough." Aside from shaking me…

"When he isn't overcome by fright. He spends most days in the stables with the horses, brushing them down, feeding them apples when he thinks no one is looking." He laughed. "I should have explained about him before our arrival."

"I daresay many other things were on our minds."

He grew sober. "Yes. Indeed."

I decided to plunge in. Perhaps if I spoke openly, he would too. I was overly tired of secrets. "I found the message that sent you away, on the floor just after you left. Forgive me, I didn't know what to do with it. You will find it inside your desk drawer—in your rooms."

He started forward and stopped apparently pleased. "I thank you."

"What did you do while away? Your leaving seemed…" Anxious? Eager? "Important."

He pressed his hands together, against his lips. "It was."

"Are you pleased with the result?"

"Elaina, perhaps in time, I will be able to tell you."

I was taken aback.

"It is better this way."

Carl came to mind. "I hope my brother does not seek to take further advantage of you."

He didn't answer but came back to the side of my bed. "I need you to trust me. Please." He willed me with his eyes. "I am going to retrieve a few novels I think you might enjoy. Is there anything else I can do to make you comfortable?"

I hesitated. His answers didn't satisfy. He seemed a caring, kind man. But what about the body? Did he mean to knowingly keep me from the truth?

"What is it?" His hand rubbed across his eyes again. "Ah yes. You've been too much alone."

Too much alone with the overflow of my life lashing against the hours. "I will be fine. I daresay we are both in need of rest."

He nodded. "You were good to Callum." He hesitated at the doorway and sent me a pleading look.

How different the world would be had the Zephyr not sailed... "I am sorry for my family—"

He strode back to my bedside with arms stiffened by his side. "Know this, Lady Elaina Sherborne. I would have paid you court with or without the Zephyr's untimely failure."

He turned on his heel and left the room, leaving me with a furious blush and a heartbeat that knocked against my chest.

He'd alluded to wanting to know me during my singular season on the carriage ride here. I didn't believe him. But could it actually be true? Did not my reduced circumstances deter him these past few years? His sudden reappearance as an investor confused me. He hadn't paid suit or even attempted conversation before the day of our wedding. What had held him back if my situation in life didn't matter? Why had he waited?

I blushed again at the flash in his eyes. I couldn't add anything up to make much sense.

A few minutes later, a maid delivered a stack of books for my perusal. "His lordship sends his compliments."

A strange disappointment arose that he'd not bothered to deliver the novels himself.

Chapter Seven

Dear Aunt Honora,

I have arrived safely to Goodwyn Abbey and am slowly growing accustomed to my new situation. I pray you are well and that Lyvia and the children are also healthy.

I feel compelled to ask you—and forgive me for pressing you on the matter—where have I heard the name of Lady Sherborne? She is an enigma. A mystery that must be solved. Lord Sherborne doesn't talk of his mother, so I do not wish to trouble him.

But why do I know her name? Now that I am safely wed, surely you can tell me. I promise to be cautious. I only want it settled in my mind. It seems I take a great lady's place—one I never dreamed of taking heretofore. I prefer to hear the truth from you before any local gossip reaches my ears.

Yours affectionately,

Elaina

I sealed the envelope with wax and wondered why Aunt Honora had not written to me before now. We had always been so close.

"You are up. Are you sure that is wise?" Zander entered our shared parlor while still tying his cravat.

"I am quite alright." Though I'd begged Nancy to tie the stays more loosely than usual. "If I stay in bed another moment longer..." I would go mad. Surely he could sense that.

"I understand." He came to my side, and studied me. "Do be careful."

Dark circles stained beneath his eyes as though his hours of sleep had been a slim respite. I wondered about the body, the man who had died. Had there been a funeral? And how far away was the kirk?

"Might I have a tour of the grounds?" I'd see where the grass had been turned over for burial and the fear that harassed me would also be put to sleep. I would rather properly reproach myself for such an imagination than condemn my new husband of a crime more heinous than my brother's.

"Only if you promise to stop if you grow too weary."

"I agree. The bruising isn't so bad, really."

"You must have been going at quite a speed to hurt yourself in such a manner."

My breath hitched. "Never again will I hurry back to bed in the dark." I attempted a laugh.

"I have some business to attend to, give me one hour?"

"Of course." I assented.

An hour passed but no Zander.

Perhaps he'd forgotten... I meandered down the stairway and peeked within the library and receiving room. Empty. He'd told me that he might be found in his study. I'd go there.

When I reached the low ceiling and doorway, I paused. Not a sound. I raised a fist and knocked softly. No answer. Maybe he didn't hear me. I slowly pushed the door open. The room was empty, but he'd been here recently. A fire simmered in the hearth and papers were strewn across the surface of the desk.

A generous portion of light shone through diamond-shaped window panes. I crossed the room to see the view and where this room was situated compared to my rooms. The stables were nearby—the garden maze nowhere to be seen.

I turned away from the window and sighed. I felt as though my life had skidded to a stop while everyone else went about their business. I had been married for a single week and my new requirements were not remotely challenging.

My eye caught handwriting on the desk. A style I well knew. Trevor's. His unique hand of hooking his lines to the left, and the distinctive way he crossed t's.

My dear, dear brother. He'd been a bastion of strength to me in those early hard days of our removal from society's graces. He'd kept us laughing and plugging forward. A furious thought plundered my mind. Why had he died rather than Carl? Trevor would have never, ever thought up such nefarious plans for me.

I lifted the letter and touched the ink across the front and saw him laughing. Tears blurred my eyes. Why had he written to Zander? And when?

"Elaina?"

Zander. "I—came looking for you, and—"

He slipped the letter from my hands as tears fell. I wiped them with my sleeve.

"It's Trevor's handwriting. I'd know it anywhere."

"It is indeed." Zander placed the letter in a drawer and locked it with a key. "I hope you did not read the contents?"

And why not? "Should I fear the contents?" A fair question.

He paused. "As you know, I had worked closely with your brothers."

"Yes. Of course." What was he hiding? "I'd give anything to have Trevor and Matthew back."

Zander squeezed his eyes and opened them again. "As would I, Elaina. As would I." He offered his arm and escorted me from the room. "Trevor was a fine man. I am more sorry than you can know that he is gone. Let's retrieve your cloak and gloves."

Enough of weary old letters. How good it felt to be out of doors! The brisk November wind swept away the remainder of my tears, and while cold, did little to stamp down my enthusiasm.

Goodwyn Abbey was far more industrious than my father's small estate had been. Everywhere I looked, young men were at work. Mending stone dykes, putting gardens to bed for the winter, exercising the horses... Sheep grazed in the distance and as far as I could see, the land belonged to Zander. Breathless wealth.

But at no point did I see upturned earth. Not even at the small, ancient chapel, whose service to humanity had long ended. Where was the poor man's grave? I pressed my hands against the lichen-covered stone and peered within. Only a leaf-littered flagstone floor and the remains of a fire. The gracious land was visible no matter which direction I looked. As though the chapel and the hills were one and the same.

Without knowing why, I closed my eyes and leaned into an old, familiar embrace. The words of a thousand prayers over as many years rose and lifted here to the God who saw all things. My pain wasn't beyond Him, nor was my confusion. This half-ruined chapel humbled me.

Zander touched my shoulder. "Are you ill, my dear?"

I opened my eyes. "On the contrary. I quite like this place." The beauty overwhelmed me.

Zander smiled and looked into his own past. "I used to camp here when I was young. Pretend to be a soldier roughing it."

"Looks as though someone has been doing the same."

"Ah, must be Callum's hide-out."

"Your tenants...they live..."

He pointed. "Down that path. We'll wait 'til you're stronger before we walk those miles. Unless you enjoy riding?"

"I've scarcely been atop a horse..." My riding lessons concluded not long before the family horses had to be sold off. The view from atop a strong horse would open the countryside to me.

"Are you averse to learning?"

"I suppose I could try." I gulped at the thought of riding the massive beasts. "I do need to meet the tenants." An excuse to force me to do what I must.

He nodded in agreement. "Indeed. They are eager to see you. They are getting rather jealous of the staff, you see." His smile was wide.

"Of the house staff? Whom I've scarcely had interaction with, so quickly they scamper from my presence?"

He grimaced. "I will speak with them."

"No—don't. I am sure they need time to adjust to a new mistress."

A chill wind blew about us and Zander gazed at me, a half-smile at his lips. "Would you like to see the stables?"

I slipped my hand back into the crook of his strong arm. Would I ever get used to the perplexing idea that I had a husband? His presence strengthened me but was I what he'd hoped for in a wife?

As we approached the stables, Callum came rushing towards me. "Lady Sherborne!" He bowed with gusto, his teeth spread wide in rapture. "Y've cum to see m' pets!"

He took my hand from Zander's and pulled me inside. Firmly, but kindly.

"Gentle with the lady, Callum." Zander followed behind.

Callum led me to the first stable. "Broonie. 'is here's Broonie."

The dark brown horse nodded her head in greeting. Callum opened his coat pocket and bade me to look within. A mischievous laugh spilled from his teeth. Apples. He held a finger to his lips and whispered in my ear. "Don't tell!"

"Already whispering secrets to the Lady, Callum?"

I grinned at the twinkle in Zander's eyes. The happiest I'd seen him since my family's disaster.

"Elaina, I see Mr. Thomhow. Can you spare me a few minutes?"

"Of course."

He smiled and left.

One of the stable boys came forward, a tow-headed youth. He bowed. "Pleased to make your acquaintance, good lady." He gave Broonie a pat. "Show her Misty-eye, Callum. Now she's a right mare."

Callum took my hand again and led me to the other end of the stable, bypassing a variety of horses, one of which I recognized from our long journey home.

"T'weren't never a finer beast." Callum shook his head. "Never, ever."

The coal black horse stood some hands higher than sweet Broonie. Her head jerked up as though she admitted my presence but only so I might admire her. In truth, I'd never seen a more beautiful animal.

Callum held an apple to her with open hands. She snatched it quickly. Then nudged his arm for more. Callum placed one of his large hands on the bridge of his nose and hummed some calming words. Misty-eye stamped her hoof and threw his hand off and turned her back to him.

"Aye, she's a fine beast," Callum withdrew, " 'at needs more pettin' t' make 'er happy. Apples without love...don't..." Callum shook his head, unable to articulate. "She can't train if she can't trust. Can't trust if she don't got love. Bein' if she'll take what's good for 'er. Aye, Misty-eye?"

"I understand." The tangible and intangible tangled together.

He moved on down the row of horses, whispering things to the beasts, feeding them apples. I slipped away to explore. Where had Zander gone? I turned past a fenced area and a few other low stone buildings and sheds. Voices rose from the other side. Zander's and Mr. Thomhow's. I paused so that I wouldn't intrude.

"We *must* make it appear as though we are still looking for him." Zander glanced behind him.

Mr. Thomhow grunted. "I think you are right."

"We ought to return again in a week—"

"Does he lie in peace?"

They spoke of the body.

I backed away from the conversation and turned toward the stables. I ran, tripping across the cobblestones and onto the green until the sore muscles protested. I held onto a stone stile to catch my breath.

"Elaina!"

I couldn't run further. My heart pounded. Panic overtook me.

Zander caught up with me. "What is it, Elaina? I saw you running. I hope Misty-eye didn't frighten you?"

I shook my head as confusion swirled. Who had they looked for and what had they found? I should have stayed to listen to Zander's answer. The young man—did he truly lie in peace? And why was he important? A deathly cold seeped into my bones.

Chapter Eight

Zander didn't wait for an answer but lifted me off the ground. "You're shivering. You've been too long outside."

Who had he held, dead, in these same arms? Fear plunged its weapon into me. I clutched his coat with one hand and held his shoulder with the other. If I should be so bold to ask—but no. If he wouldn't tell me about his secret dealings with Carl and Trevor...then I doubt he would tell me what I most needed to know. My heart pounded uncontrollably and I couldn't stop shaking. How was I ever going to know for sure? That he was good enough for me to trust?

A side door opened before us as Zander carried me into his office and settled me into his chair. The footman and Molly followed us within.

"Molly—hot coffee, please. Samuel, fetch the doctor."

"I don't need the doctor."

Zander threw a blanket around my legs and rubbed my hands between his. "My dear, you certainly do." Such a decent man. His solidity begged me to tolerate what I didn't understand. Yet the unknown chafed at the wounds already in place.

Dr. Rillian stepped in even before the coffee had arrived. Did he live so close? Apparently so. His hair was askew and his spectacles dangled from one ear when he arrived.

Clearly, he'd rushed over. "Lady Sherborne. What have we here?"

"Over exhaustion, I think." Zander stood.

"Not at all." I disagreed. If only I might speak openly. What would happen if I did? My pulse raced harder.

Zander gestured. "See how her cheeks are flushed?"

"Hmm?" The doctor adjusted his spectacles. "No more than yours." He took my wrist. "You haven't been running, have you?"

"I…"

The doctor glanced at Zander. "How does it feel?" He gestured toward my mid-section. "Bruising better?"

"Much. Hardly any discomfort."

Doctor Rillian took a coffee from Molly's tray and gulped it down. "I'll take more of that, if you please."

"Should she not rest?" Zander queried.

"Do you want to rest, Lady Sherborne?"

I shook my head, but in truth, I didn't know. Too many thoughts and questions distracted from sorting my desires.

Zander was at a loss. "Then what could be wrong?" If only he knew.

"Who said anything is wrong? She's fit as a fiddle." He leaned in and whispered to Zander. "If I were you, I'd ask the lady myself." He saluted like a captain and left the room.

I had to agree with the doctor's orders.

Zander said nothing, but poured a cup of coffee, added a generous portion of cream, and put it in my hands. "Drink up." He paced for a few minutes while I cradled the hot brew, then slid a footrest beneath my feet.

I took a sip of the coffee and swallowed, every nerve tingling.

He perched on the edge of his desk and folded his arms. "You were running from something. If it wasn't a fear of horses, what scared you?"

I steeled myself for any fate. Finally. I would tell him everything. No longer could I hide behind deceptive clouds or false fronts. "The message. The secretive way in which you left. The body you carried within the night you came home..."

He jerked to his feet, eyes wide.

"And Trevor's message, locked away in that drawer. I don't understand, Lord Sherborne." I couldn't bring myself to call him Zander. "I don't understand why such devastation has visited my family and why the secrets still abound." I wiped an errant tear. "Learning of Carl's intentions concerning me has left me near speechless—yet you were willing enough to tell me the truth about that indignity."

"I thought you already knew." His mouth remained set.

"What am I supposed to think? You are kind and bid me to be at peace. You've protected me from an evil I cannot fathom. But what does the rest of it mean? Why did I see you carry a body into our house?" I shook again, as uncontrollable fear had overtaken me. "And why must you pretend to look for someone?"

"You overheard my conversation with Mr. Thomhow."

"Part of it."

He knelt down on the rug beside my chair. "I am sorry, Elaina. There are things I cannot explain. The less you know, the better."

"You must understand, Lord Sherborne, that I am unused to intrigue of any kind other than my sister's elopement four years ago. Last month I was wiping dust from the pianoforte, mending Aunt Honora's gloves, and teaching Sunday school. Definitely and absolutely *not* watching my new husband carry a body into Goodwyn Abbey." I trembled so, the coffee sloshed from my cup.

He took it from my hands and set it aside. "I did carry someone within. Not a body, but someone who needed care." His expression was grave. "And still needs it."

He wasn't dead as I supposed? "Who is it?"

He shook his head. "I cannot tell you."

"But why?"

"Trust me." His eyes implored me. "You *must* trust me. I am doing all I can to keep you safe."

Aside from my brother's machinations, what did he mean? "Did not our marriage already achieve this?"

"I had hoped so. But—" he struggled. "There is more I cannot tell, more that you don't know."

"You don't trust me." Yet he asked this of me.

"I wouldn't have married you if I couldn't trust you."

"How did you know you could?" I shook my head. "We scarcely—"

"I had a sense about you a long time ago."

There it was again... "Yet, our exceedingly short acquaintance."

"Indeed." He stood and walked over to his desk. "I have a modicum of faith, like you. And then there was this." He unlocked the drawer and removed the letter he locked away earlier. "And in that good faith, I suppose I can let you read it."

My heart lurched.

He slowly walked back to my chair as though still deciding if it was a good idea. "This is a secret I don't have to keep, though I beg you to keep it to yourself. It is no one's business but ours."

I held Trevor's letter in my hands and trembled once again. Zander stood at the fireplace, with arms folded. He wanted me to trust him—maybe this letter would help.

I unfolded the paper and read:

Lord Sherborne,

You have my utmost thanks for your promise. If what I fear does indeed come to fruition, I may find myself powerless to care for my family. I do not worry for my son, as I know he is sagacious and will make a way for himself. Perhaps at sea. My sister, as we have discussed, has no one else. By marrying her, you will have eased my mind considerably. I worry for her the most. She is good and trustworthy, of this you can be certain.

Would that I could trust my brother as much as I do her. When you approached me about a potential courtship, I was surprised. Our later conversations and your consistently upright decisions confirmed that she could not do better. And so I sought this pledge from you, and not without much prayer and supplication. Lord willing, our suspicions will prove for naught and you may take your time courting her as she welcomes you, you know I will not object.

Praying without ceasing,
Trevor Dawes

I was quiet for a moment, trying to sort everything in my mind. Trevor feared an occasion that would prevent his care for me—that much was clear. Was almost as if he knew he was going to die. But surely, he didn't! Surely, if he knew the Zephyr would be wrecked, he would have stayed far away. Maybe he suspected the impending failure and debtor's prison or—my imagination failed to fill in the blank. In any case, despite Carl's reprehensible scheming for his own survival, Trevor and Zander had made a plan for my welfare. Even while I had no idea of the need for such assistance.

Zander looked at me. Heat flooded my face. Our marriage had to be rushed because of Carl's duplicity. Zander had been telling the truth all along, only we hadn't been given enough time, and I, no margin for choice in the matter.

I looked back down at Trevor's beautiful handwriting. Carl hadn't sealed my fate, Trevor had. With much prayer and supplication, he'd written this confirmation. I traced my finger over the inky words. His last grand gift to me—a husband.

I recalled the night before he sailed. I helped him pack his bag. I'd sneaked in a tin of shortbread, which he'd discovered before leaving the house. Crumbs clung to his coat.

I approached him, hands on my hips. "You've been found out, brother."

"I don't know what you mean?"

From the twinkle in his eye, he most certainly did. I swiped his coat clean and took his hat from the hook. "I will miss you and Matthew. I know it's only for a few weeks, but Aunt Honora is too easy to beat at chess. I'd much rather defeat you."

He took my hands and smiled. "I love you, dear sister. Pray for us."

"Always."

Days later, in the upward wind of my prayers, he and Matthew went with them.

Trevor trusted Zander...

Zander pulled his desk chair next to mine and sank into the seat. I folded the words away and handed it back to him. He set it back on his desk as though a sacred contract.

He tented his fingers and looked at me over them. "I always intended a proper courtship—more time—a chance to become acquainted with you, as I'd long desired."

"I should have liked that." I'd calmed. Trevor's words had been an unexpected balm, though I hated that even then, he couldn't trust Carl. Why hadn't I sensed the truth? His written words were only a sketch. Trevor hadn't told me anything.

"I wonder why Trevor did not confide in me." The slight stung.

"He didn't want you to worry. We hoped we were wrong..."

"And if I were told of the situation...my knowledge would somehow bring risk to me."

Zander nodded. "A risk, no matter how small, I was not willing to take. Too many lives have already been lost. You are grieving, why must you suffer more?"

I covered his hand with mine. "I am indebted to you."

"No—"

"But I am." My voice cracked.

He squeezed my hand. "We can still enjoy a courtship…"

I lifted my eyes to his. Hope filled his face.

For this grace, Lord, I thank thee…

Chapter Nine

A few days later, Zander invited me to dinner downstairs. His intent was clear—he meant to court me and be a good husband all at once. And with each solitary step I took down the long stairway, I knew I'd never be able to return to days of innocence. Of not knowing. My cherished brother had thought of my welfare even when we tottered on disaster's brink. And Zander, this confusing hero of mine, sought to fulfill a promise and protected me by carefully keeping secrets. It begged another question. How much danger yet lurked? Was Zander safe? Could we ever be?

"Truth will out," as Father used to say. And I must patiently wait for it. Would the full facts be even more difficult to bear?

Zander waited at the foot of the stairs, appreciation in his gaze. Nancy helped me dress my hair and don my black silk evening gown. I'd not had the occasion to wear it for a few years and had forgotten how it made me feel.

"You are lovely this evening." He offered his arm—would I ever grow accustomed to touching the firm muscle beneath his jacket, or his large, warm hands? I'd become a blushing debutante again. He led me to the dining room. The long table had been set for two. Candelabras glowed, wine had been poured. He pulled my chair and I sat.

"I wondered if you used the dining room."

He smiled. "Hard to eat alone in a large space."

"I suppose it would be." I'd never had such singular meals—with only one person. My daily table consisted of Aunt Honora, Trevor, and Matthew. Carl and his family took their meals in the upper portion of our townhome. I'd occasionally join the delightful menagerie with my nieces and nephews... Every moment they were missed.

The footman quietly served the soup. The silver, perfectly polished and initialed with a scrolled "S" on every piece. The china, very fine in blue and white with an orange floral design, captured my interest.

"Should you like to choose your own pattern, Elaina?"

"Any bride might enjoy doing so." His question touched me.

His eyes twinkled. "We are in Staffordshire, you know. Much to choose from."

I touched the rim of the plate. I couldn't remember the last time I'd chosen anything for myself besides the occasional cut of beef. "I confess I rather like what sits before me." The design was delicate, beautiful.

"Do you?"

"Indeed. I have no complaint."

"The colors are to your liking?"

"They are vibrant and interesting. Did these belong to your mother?"

"An anniversary gift from my father—he picked them out for her. She was never happy using anything else."

He spoke of his mother...had Aunt Honora received my letter? Where was her response?

The entrée arrived, thin slices of chicken swimming in a savory cream sauce. The cook had outdone herself. I must remember to send my compliments.

"There is something I need to discuss with you." He took a sip of wine and continued. "Mrs. Thomhow is biting at the chomp to shop with you."

The image of the sweet, red-haired woman wearing a horse's bridle sent an unbidden giggle up my throat. How long had it been since I laughed? "Shopping?" I scarcely understood the concept!

"She thinks that my bride ought to have ten new gowns, no exceptions."

I dropped my fork and looked down at my out-of-date evening dress. My gowns couldn't be called fashionable. Patched and resewn more times than I could count. They wouldn't do to play the part of Lady Sherborne. What an embarrassment I would be.

"My trousseau—I—they—" my words came out in a jumble. It was all I had. Flames rose as my pride and vanity dueled for dominance. My clothing could not be helped.

"Elaina." Zander leaned forward. "I did not mean to humiliate. You would be beautiful in whatever you wore."

He called me beautiful...I pulled my eyes from his. I couldn't help being flattered. I hadn't heard those words in a very long time. I'd once thought too much of my looks. Thought they could overcome the deficits of my dowry.

During my season, I'd been called beautiful on many occasions, and I believed each man. Until months went by and no one came calling. I'd looked into the mirror at my visage at every angle, wondering what threw them off. Surely some of my suitors would come back. What was it about me that countered their recent conquests? Hard lessons were learned about what being "cut" from society meant. It hurt worse than a physical injury.

Before then, I'd purchased a few new gowns every single season. No exception. But I'd learned to cast away those expectations along with my obsession for skin-deep beauty.

Zander crooked a half-smile. "My favorite is the blue one." His hand took mine and squeezed.

"The blue one?" My voice quaked. "I haven't worn it since—" It was my oldest gown. Well-made and still serviceable.

"I confess, I saw you in it when you did not see me. You were teaching children when I met with the vicar." His hand pressed mine. "How you taught them, and treated them with love and respect—perhaps showing more care than their busy mothers—it was then, Elaina, that I first desired to court you."

Emotion caught in my throat. "So not when I tramped your foot at the theater?" A poor attempt at humor.

Still, he smiled. "Well," he shrugged, "Circumstances prevented me from many pursuits for a while."

"Circumstances?"

He smiled but did not expound. "Elaina, as Lady Sherborne, you must see that the local shops are blessed by our patronage. The draper and his wife have seven children to care for, three of them are her nieces. It is imperative that you order no less than ten gowns."

Understanding dawned. Delight as well. "I am ridiculous."

"And do purchase whatever else you may require." He released my hand and pulled a box from his pocket and slid it towards my plate. "You aren't ridiculous, I applaud your recent economies. You bore your situation with far greater elegance than anyone I know in Town would."

"You call patched dresses "elegant"?"

"If you are the one wearing them, yes." He looked at the box and then me. "Open it."

I picked it up and lifted the lid. Resting atop black velvet was a bracelet that matched my wedding ring. A gold circlet, with an oval ruby at the center. Simple and stunning.

"Your wedding present." He lifted the bracelet out and wrapped it around my pulsing wrist. "I meant to gift it to you sooner..."

A loud giggle came from the doorway.

"Callum?" Zander turned in his chair.

The giggle sounded again as his large feet shuffled to our table. "More flowers for Lady Sherborne," he laughed again, "In case the old ones shrivel, hee-hee-hee." He made a failed effort to be quiet.

Another newspaper flower bouquet was presented to me, this time roses. "How did you know that I love roses?"

He shrugged and smiled.

Zander waved him to a chair. "Sit, Callum. Have some supper with us."

Callum shook his head. "Ate with cook. Had pudding with Broonie."

One of Zander's brows rose. "You didn't feed Broonie your pudding did you?"

Callum looked down and shyly scooted backward before scampering out of the door.

"He is a dear."

"Feeds the horses too many apples. Sometimes I fear that they'll all come down with colic.

I laughed and Zander joined me. I couldn't help it. I thought I'd been sinking into the darkest of darkness, but here sat the hero, and abiding with him, a delightful young man.

Might there be other people to live for and love besides my lost and divided family? The ring on my finger and bracelet around my wrist winked a truth. My new family.

"Thank you, Zander."

He leaned his chin on his hand for a long time, looking at me. The footman had to clear his throat so he could serve dessert, a delicate raspberry tart.

The rest of the evening passed amicably, I think we were both surprised. As though we'd been holding our breath and had finally come up for air. We were almost at ease in each other's company.

That night, however, I dreamt that someone cried. Callum was lost in his dreaded woods—a distant scream slipped from the thin air and became a whimper down my own throat. I awoke, disturbed. I was relieved when morning light lifted away the night. I crawled from bed, slipped my robe about my shoulders, and stood before the hot coals in the fireplace.

Poor Callum. I wonder how often he had nightmares. Someone once said that children blessedly have short memories. I am not so certain that is correct.

A soft knock came to my door and Nancy carried in some tea.

"Where is Callum's room located, Nancy?"

"Pardon, ma'am. He has a room two doors down from Lord Sherborne, but rarely sleeps inside."

"Where then?"

Nancy shrugged. "One can never predict, though he's often been found in the stables. Sometimes he takes the small bedroom by the kitchen. It's set up with a cot for emergencies."

"I fear he endured nightmares last night."

Nancy looked at me and shook her head. "Not that I know of, Lady Sherborne. I didn't hear him, and my room's closest to the kitchen and the stable both." She curtsied on her way out. "Maybe he finally slept in his own bed last night. That would be a wonder."

Molly entered and helped me dress for the day. What was in the large box she carried? "New cloak's been sent to you, my lady." She lifted out the fine dark brown wool and spread it across the bed. Green silk lined the interior, a pair of brown leather gloves to match. "I've been asked to tell you that the carriage leaves at nine o'clock."

I dressed in my better walking gown with my hair in a simple bun for the bonnet. How silly I would appear in the village, in that old bonnet, dress, and shoes covered by new cloak and gloves.

Zander's words about beauty and elegance came to mind…it did not matter. I must swallow my pride. I stepped into the parlor for breakfast just as he was reentering his room. He paused when he heard me and doubled back, leaving his bedroom door wide open.

"Good morning, Elaina." He was dressed for business, it seemed. Handsome. His eyes, though, bore hints of exhaustion. Callum must have awakened him as well. Or was it the man he'd carried into Goodwyn? The mysterious guest.

"Good morning."

He slowed his approach when he reached me. "Hate to leave you to breakfast alone, I do have business to attend to. Forgive me?"

I nodded. Aunt Honora and I often breakfasted alone as Trevor went to the offices early and Matthew to school. Even so, being solitary at the morning meal felt strange.

"Don't let me keep you." From work? Secrets? Both?

He reached a hand to my cheek as though reading my mind. He pressed a kiss to my forehead that sent fire all the way to my fingertips. He stepped back and formally bowed as though we were at a ball. Then left me alone.

We were indeed attending a dance together. One in which he courted me while wisely skirting dangers I couldn't see.

I had no choice but to follow his firm lead.

Chapter Ten

Mrs. Thomhow met me at the foot of the stairs wreathed in smiles.

"How are the children doing?"

"Much improved, my dear. Thank you for your kind message." She squeezed my hands.

"My sister-in-law was always busiest when the children were ill. A constant challenge, to be sure."

"I confess, removing myself from the confines of my house is much needed." She looped her arm in mine as we made our way outside. "Mr. Thomhow is on duty today. He will no doubt have them jumping in bed and all manner of antics. And this once I will turn a blind eye," she laughed.

"I so look forward to meeting them." We turned toward the coach and I was surprised by Zander at the door, wearing a high hat—a tall and foreboding aspect if he hadn't been smiling.

"Ready?" His smile was irresistible.

I felt the kiss he'd left on my forehead but two hours prior. "I am." He handed me inside, then Mrs. Thomhow, and settled on opposite seat. "You're coming with us?"

"Someone has to pay for the damage about to ensue." His lips quirked a smile and Mrs. Thomhow threw her head back and laughed. "I leave no shop with any outstanding credit if I can help it."

I looked away. Creditors had forever come calling on the Dawes family. A little window positioned to view the front door made the perfect place to spy out the caller. I knew when to answer and when to hide in my room and ignore the ringing bell, I am ashamed to say. Not that I've ever had control of any expenses outside of putting food on the table.

Cold facts. Zander had paid those debts for me.

Mrs. Thomhow tightened her wrap about her shoulders. "Are you ready to be stared at, pointed to, and whispered about for the rest of the day?"

I looked to Zander. "Is our story already well known?"

"No."

Mrs. Thomhow sent me a knowing smile. "You are the new Lady Sherborne, dear. Every shop you enter and every word you utter will be bandied about the village."

Zander tossed her an annoyed glance. "You are scaring her, Mrs. Thomhow."

"Better she knows than be shocked by ridiculous gossip."

Would such things never end? "I am no stranger to the tarnishing effects of gossip."

Mrs. Thomhow patted my hand. "I'm sorry to hear it. And don't worry—won't matter much anyhow. No one really takes them seriously—except for when…" Her voice trailed off and Zander stiffened.

I looked from the window at the rolling countryside, stone fences and ancient trees grown high amid fields. At a bend in the road, I saw the village, nestled between protective hills. The church spire rising from the center.

"Butterton." Zander said.

We drew closer. Every building, from home, to barn, to shop seemed to be made of stone. A stream flowed through it with ancient footbridges arching over in various locations. A far cry from London's brick and timber, hustle and bustle, and the mighty river Thames.

The carriage drew up to a shop and stopped. The apothecary. Mrs. Thomhow gathered her belongings. "Won't be long. I'll meet you at the drapers." The door opened and a footman handed her down.

Zander filled her seat and leaned in. "Don't worry, Elaina. They will love you. Pay no mind to the gossip."

"How can you possibly know that I'll make such a positive impression?"

He pulled a large wallet from his coat and wagged it in the air, "Because they will put many good meals on the table as a result of your shopping." He handed me a few pounds. "And I daresay, they'd like more business in the future."

I'd not held a pound note in years. I tucked it within my reticule and pulled the strings tight, wondering what kind of gossip had affected the Sherbornes—what had Mrs. Thomhow been alluding to?

The carriage stopped again, this time, in front of the drapers. Bolts of brightly-colored cloth filled the widow. A little girl stopped sweeping and ran within, no doubt alerting her parents to our arrival.

"I worry I will spend too much."

"No economizing today, my dear. And do get fitted for a riding habit." He winked.

"Riding..." Whatever was he thinking?

If he could afford such expenses—my mind wandered. He'd been my brother's greatest investor and sent provision to my family in exchange for—I stopped the thought. I couldn't grasp his wealth and abilities, regardless of the losses caused by Dawes Shipping's failure.

The door opened and Zander handed me out and into the shop we went. Introductions were made. The kind, narrow-faced woman and her amiable husband put me at ease immediately.

Zander took my hand and bowed. "I leave you to their care. Mrs. Thomhow will be along presently. I'll be back in an hour."

He was leaving me? Again?

"Wait." I tugged his hand.

"Yes?"

I remembered he liked the blue dress. Did I care to please him in this regard? He led me to a corner for more privacy, yet shyness had overtaken me. "I don't know how to begin."

"What are your favorite colors?"

I turned the question around. "What are yours?" I looked at what he wore, a black coat over a blue and gold striped waistcoat.

"All of them." He winked and left me bewildered.

The draper's wife appeared at my elbow. "Now then, Lady Sherborne. What will ye have?"

I took a deep breath and offered a generous smile. Time to fill my wardrobe as I'd never done before. I was a lady now.

Mrs. Thomhow joined soon after and became the best of advisors. Well over two hours later, cloth and patterns were chosen. I'd been measured. A stack of new undergarments sat in a basket, modestly behind the desk, and muslins for new nightgowns were already being cut from the bolts.

Mrs. Thomhow clapped her hands together. "Silks and wool?"

"Here, ma'am." Stockings were added to the pile.

"Now then, on to the haberdashery."

A well-dressed woman was there, with a younger copy beside her, giving directions for bonnets that would suit a high hair arrangement. They fastened their glances upon me with interest, took in every part of my clothing with scanning eyes. I nodded to admit their strange perusal and moved to the other side of the shop, but not without hearing over-loud whispers follow my back.

"As bewitched as Lady Sherborne was, I don't wonder her son being afflicted with the same…"

"Hush." The older admonished the younger.

They obviously knew who I was.

Mrs. Thomhow offered me a smile and spoke in a low tone. "News traveled fast." She looked toward the two gawkers.

"Indeed." But what did the young woman mean by calling Zander's mother bewitched? With an affliction? I set the thought aside and fulfilled my lady-like duty.

After various bonnets were chosen, I was more than glad to leave the stifling shop and those inspecting eyes. Thankfully, Zander met us on the walk. "My apologies, ladies." He offered his arm to me, "Elaina—come see."

Mrs. Thomhow curtsied, "Please excuse me, I'm having tea with an old friend." She took her leave while Zander led me to the stables but a minute's walk from the shop.

He stopped in front of a striking white horse. Both tall and regal. So that's what he'd been doing. "You did order a riding habit I hope?" He smiled.

My jaw dropped.

"My wedding present to you."

"You already gave me…"

"Well, here's another. Here, say hello to Niveus." He took my hand and placed it on the beast's nose, soft and warm.

She leaned into my touch and took a deep breath. Her appraisal of me was far more friendly than the two strangers at the shop. "It is too much."

"No, it isn't. Not when there are many tenants to visit on Goodwyn land. I intend for you to come with me when I make the next rounds." He gave Niveus a pat. "You'll need a good horse to do that."

Excitement rose. "I've been desirous of meeting them." I turned to face him. "You've given me much," I whispered for fear of being overheard.

"You are my wife. What I have is yours." He led me out of the stables.

All that he has?

"We are to luncheon with the vicar—he is anxious to make your acquaintance. He is the kind of vicar I think you might approve of."

"Meaning, he takes his occupation seriously—and doesn't read a cold, dusty sermon from an old book?"

"That and he matches his words with comparable actions."

"I am glad of it."

"You may also be glad to know that he is good friends with the one who wedded us."

I nodded. "And you, Zander, do you take your faith seriously?" The risky question flew from my mouth before I could control it. I couldn't retract.

He stopped our walk and looked deeply into my eyes. "Utterly."

To be a good friend of Trevor's, one would also be a friend of God's. I should have guessed. Especially given the words in the letter Trevor had written about me. *With much prayer and supplication...*

I expected a twin of the dear, gentle vicar I'd left behind in London but met with a rugged, brawny man of quick wit and bold opinion. The fork he dipped into his steak pie cut the crust in one swipe and swallowed in the next breath. I thought his sharp eyes might snap me in two.

"What say you, Lady Sherborne? Does your station in life make you a better person? Better than anyone else in this humble village?" A muscle twitched around his eye.

The audacity! "I know it does not."

"How so exactly?"

My answer did not satisfy. I searched for words. "Nothing can make me better outside of Christ's work in me. It isn't a question of who or what station in life is "better", is it? Or how I measure up to others... But the question is: what has God called me to do, and am I doing it? No station can raise me, not even if I were queen, to the heights of His regard except for my obedience to Him. Nor can any station in life create contentment aside from this."

The vicar leaned back in his chair. "So you'd willingly be a fishmonger's wife and still be happy?"

"You did not ask a question regarding happiness."

"In most cases better means happier."

"A fishmonger's wife can be better—even than her so-called betters, find contentment if not happiness."

The vicar took a huge bite and spoke through his food. "Well-said. I've known such a woman."

Zander had grown quiet. Had I said the wrong thing in his thinking? Little I could do to change it.

The vicar pulled his napkin from his collar and drained his cider. "Lord Sherborne, I approve. You've made an excellent choice. I pray her ladyship excuses my forthrightness. You've much serving to do from your height. Occasionally you will have to bend quite low."

"I hope, Reverend, that I can do less bending and more serving from my knees. I don't care to appear to stoop—they will know it."

He waved a fork in the air. "Even stooping won't erase your title."

"Does a title need erasing while serving from my knees? I hope to do it honor, if there's any power or glory found in it, it will belong to God for His use."

"You've married a theologian, Lord Sherborne." He folded his arms and shook his head. "Don't tell me you are one of those rare ladies who can also cook."

"Well..." I laughed.

Zander looked at me with surprise on his face.

"Bread baking is a favorite pastime."

The vicar tossed his chin up. "And what will you do, dear woman, if you must do your serving at the heights befitting your title? Will you despise them and prefer your knees?"

I lay down my fork. "I suppose in that case..." I paused. I never thought to be the wife of a baron. "I hope that I wouldn't despise the gentry, as they are too, made in the image of God." I've had to forgive the Ton, over and over until it became second nature. Their betrayal had become nothing but chaff in the wind. Eventually, the forgiveness came easily. I didn't have to beg God for it anymore, He'd left it within me as a natural response. But engaging them further? After everything? I thought of Carl and my stomach clenched.

"Your brow is wrinkled. I've stumbled onto something."

Zander touched my hand beneath the table.

The vicar nodded his head, his voice gentled. "I understand, my Lady. More than you know. For the fortitude to serve them, you must reach even higher. Tis always the answer. It is easy to serve those whose needs are food and clothing. The challenge is to help them that seem to have everything. Pah. But it must be done. As you well know, they don't have everything after all..." He stood. "I have tested you long enough, and no doubt your husband is ready to wring my neck. He will apologize the entire road home, I imagine."

Zander stood with hands palms out. "You gave her a rather pointed dose of conversation." Was that mild annoyance? His lips curved upward, but a line formed between his brows.

I stood as well. "You are quite engaging, Reverend."

"My tongue gets the better of me." He smiled wide, not a bit sorry. He leaned towards Zander's ear as though I couldn't hear. "You might tell that new wife anything—and—" his brows lifted and his lips drew into a line, "everything. If you get my drift."

He shook Zander's hand and we took our leave.

What did he know? More than I? Likely.

Zander wasted no time. "Elaina, he was in rare form today. I do apologize."

I laughed. "Not at all. I like him. He doesn't put on pretenses. He doesn't make one guess at what he is thinking or feeling." Or doing.

"An uncommon man to be sure." Zander looked down at me. "You spoke as I have never heard another woman speak."

I shook my head, afraid of having been misunderstood. "I am sorry if I said too much..."

His brows pulled together as we stopped in front of the carriage. "I meant what I said. I am thankful to be wed to someone such as you." He offered a soft smile as handed me into the carriage where twine-tied paper packages brimmed from the seats.

I rode home alone as Zander needed to ride Niveus alongside us. Mrs. Thomhow stayed behind and would retrieve more of my purchases by the next evening. The drapers would stitch for me through the night.

I closed my eyes and leaned against the velvet interior, wondering at the new life I'd been handed. Of stooping low and raising high. Of village whispers and nagging memories...

Chapter Eleven

Three letters had arrived. Zander's desk had been cleared and the missives sat in a row. He motioned to a seat and sat on the opposite side.

"The first one is from Butterton Hall. We are invited to dinner—I suspect they are curious to meet you. We will probably accept, if that is amenable to you?"

"I should enjoy making their acquaintance."

He tapped the envelope. "One can never tell what kind of evening it will be or what mood Lady Camden will be in. However, it is a connection you should make as Lady Sherborne."

"Of course." This societal expectation did not surprise.

Zander turned over the next letter—Aunt Honora's graceful handwriting listed my name.

"I wondered that she had not written to me." I reached for it but Zander's hand covered mine. The fire of his touch matched the flame in his eyes.

"Do you trust her, Elaina?"

Should I? I'd never been given a reason not to trust her. I did wrestle with the fact that she knew Carl's plan for me but never breathed a word of warning. But maybe she'd been working all along to keep me from the unpleasantness. I think that is exactly what she'd done. I must think well of her.

"I do trust her."

He removed his hand. "If there is anything within her message that gives you pause, will you promise to tell me?"

"Yes." I remembered what I'd asked of her. Things about his mother. I gulped at the thought that Zander might have opened the letter without my permission. What would he think of me if he knew of my intimate inquiries?

"That brings us to the final letter sent to you." He flipped this one over. "From Carl."

I recoiled.

"With your permission, I should like to read it first."

I nodded. Did Carl think me ignorant of what he'd tried to do? I trembled and moved towards the crackling fire. What could he possibly have to say to me? How could he write and pretend to be the least bit brotherly after his behavior?

Zander read and with a final grunt, set the letter down and joined me at the fire. "He complains of his work, his salary, the sum of his recent annuity."

"It has only been a few weeks since he was saved from the poor house. How could he possibly complain?"

"Do you want to read the letter?"

"Is there anything about Lyvia and the children?"

He shook his head and snatched the letter from his desk. "You should read it anyway. Best you know."

With all that was in me, I didn't want to. I looked down at the words and scanned them. He hoped I was happily settled. But continued in such a way that he meant to throw guilt upon my good fortune. In hopes that I would send him more funds? I thrust them away from me. I didn't understand this version of Carl. He was a stranger.

Bitterness rose. "I wonder why you helped him."

His eyes latched onto mine. "Do you wonder? Truly?"

Because of him, the children wouldn't starve. And I was kept out of harm's way.

His hand came under my chin and his thumb stroked my jaw. He said nothing and gazed at me. My attraction to him had been growing. I'd wanted to deny it. It made me feel wild and out of control. What if I did give him my heart? That's what a courting couple was wont to do. Yet, what if I didn't know enough—what if the truths he withheld shattered my heart? Like Carl?

He bent his head closer to mine, his lips a whisper away. My heart pounded with the full truth of what I did know. For certain. I wanted to love this man.

Footsteps scuffed along the hall and a rush of cool air swirled between us—we quickly drew apart.

"My pardon, Lord Sherborne, Lady Sherborne."

Zander rubbed his jaw. "Mr. Thomhow?"

He held up a large book. "The ledger you requested?"

My face warmed.

His brows rose above a pair of spectacles. "Should I come back later?"

"Five minutes?"

"Make that fifteen. I'll have coffee brought in."

The door shut behind him leaving us alone once again.

I looked down at my boots. If I looked up, if I faced him—would I still see desire? Would he?

"Elaina?" He begged my attention as both hands reached to cradle my face. "Have I frightened you?"

Frightened me? Indeed. I was terrified. "No." My answer broke in a tremble.

He pulled me into his arms and held me. I wanted to weep at his tenderness and the sound of his heart thumping as hard as mine beneath his solid chest. Because I was near?

I wished the fear would go away. That trust might triumph. Is that where faith came in? I pulled back and rose to my toes and kissed his clean-shaven jaw.

He eyed the door. "Best see that Callum isn't feeding Niveus too many..." His words trailed off.

"Apples. Yes." I turned to go but he caught my hand and pulled me back.

"You are incredibly..." He didn't finish. He gave as I had, a burning reminder on my cheek that we were meant to share a lasting love.

Mr. Thomhow and coffee arrived and I fled to the stables. I'd forgotten Aunt Honora's letter on his desk.

Later, when the afternoon's blush had cooled and the dark of night had grown colder, I made my way back inside Goodwyn to prepare for dinner—and to snatch the letter I'd left behind.

Mrs. Thomhow waylaid me as I was about to turn the corner to the study.

"How timely, dear." She gestured toward my room. "Some of the things you ordered have arrived."

"Already?"

"Including your riding habit." Her eyes smiled.

I would have to relearn how to ride. The few times I'd indulged had been on old, slow beasts—not a graceful horse like Niveus.

"Let's view the plunder, shall we?"

The letter must come later...

Nancy was in my room unwrapping the dear creations. The draper and his wife and some of his daughters had worked their fingers to the bone. There, across the bed, was the blue gown I'd asked to be fashioned after my old one. The one Zander had seen me in, that I planned to wear this eve.

When he arrived at our evening meal, he seemed flustered. In naught but a shirtwaist and rumpled sleeves, he hadn't taken time to groom himself, while I, in a rather silly state of mind, had become absorbed with my self-care.

He shoveled a few bites of potatoes in his mouth and downed a glass of water. Chimes rang from the small mantle clock. His head jerked to check the time.

"In a hurry?"

"I've business to attend to."

"So late in the day? Can it not wait?" I fear I sounded like a true wife then, the hint of a nag on my tongue. I didn't fancy being left alone yet again.

His glacial eyes captured mine and dashed away. "It cannot."

I stood. "Don't let me keep you, Zander."

His chewing slowed as his gaze settled on me fully. "You chose blue." A smile lifted his lips. "I completely approve."

The door burst open and Doctor Rillian strode in. "Imperative you come."

Zander tossed his napkin to the ground and followed the doctor. I hadn't even seen him ride in. Did he tend the sick man we couldn't mention? He must.

I peeked around the door, tempted to follow. Was safer, he'd said, for me not to know the whole of it. It didn't seem right. Why couldn't he tell me? I was sure not to know the man, so why did it matter? Indeed, my circle of acquaintances was small and those of true friends even smaller.

My spirits sank. If Zander was going to be busy, I'd retrieve my letter. I quietly walked downstairs and into the study without notice. A small fire still glowed lending enough light to see by. I stepped to the desk. There—on near the edge. I felt for the wax seal. It had been opened.

I shut my eyes. *No*.

I hoped upon hope that Aunt had ignored my query this once. How flighty it would seem to ask for gossip concerning my departed mother-in-law. But why had he opened it? Or better question – why not? I told him that I trusted her. I did not fear anything she had to say.

I rushed back to my room, sat by the light, and read the letter.

My Dear Niece,

The weeks since you've been gone from us have been long and strange. It is not the same place you left behind—not without you, Trevor, and Matthew. Half of our household has departed, and you, the dearest. Lyvia and the children do well, your marriage sees them fed, though my dear, I do wish we had funds to pay for a governess and a nurse. Lyvia relies on me to teach the oldest girls French, though I hardly see what good it will do them if they are not allowed to enter into society as they deserve. Unless, of course, they meet with the same fortune as you...with such a connection to a baron, I dare hope.

What I did not relay to you before your marriage—and what I will relay to you now may not have any value. As a fallen family, you must give it little account. Just before the Dawes family received the irrevocable cut from the Ton, Lady Sherborne endured a dark intrigue as well. While too valuable to truly be cut as we've been—the family suffered gossip of the worst sort. It was said, forgive me, dear, that Lady Sherborne bore a gypsy child which she allowed the Sherborne name and to wander the halls. The story changed a few times, I will not regale you with such drivel. However, the topic of gossip proved too painful for Lord and Lady Sherborne to bear and so they took themselves entirely from society. Their absence, unfortunately, seemed to give credence to the stories. Zander's ability to make a strong match deteriorated. The family, it was said, had been bewitched by the gypsies.

I never once believed these ill-told words. Those of Sherborne ilk would not associate with gypsies except to hie them away from their land, as is fitting. I believe the gossip had started when (if you were here and I were speaking this aloud, I'd have the children close their ears) Lady Sherborne received unwanted advances from one rather close to the throne. In this case, God bless King George, but what can anyone say against the word of a Duke and that of his Duchess? This I learned from my former lady's maid who was a friend of Lady Sherborne's maid.

Surely you do not mind these intrigues, dear. I didn't want to bother you with them but thought it fair for you to know since perhaps you are thinking of reentering society and find the water cold in places. The gossip has died down for the most part and I daresay a baron and his wife would be welcome almost anywhere!

The cook is making beef roast today and Lyvia, dear that she is, never learned to play chess. You are missed.

Much love,

Aunt Honora

I sagged against the chair, sickened. Why had I thought that my memory tugged at something important? This disgusting gossip did not satisfy. Aunt Honora spoke of Callum.

Someone got wind of his existence within Goodwyn Abbey and twisted the care given him into something rude and coarse. Lord and Lady Sherborne had taken the abandoned child within the loving fold of their home and kept him safe. Anyone could tell he'd spent happy years here. If Aunt Honora visited me, would she too think the worst?

I would speak to Zander about it. Perhaps if I were honest about this letter—since it did appear he'd read it—he would be at ease to share more information with me. Even his darkest secrets. How could knowing possibly hurt anyone?

I knew some men who didn't think a woman's brain capable of hard truths. I never understood how safety might be found in ignorance.

I dressed for bed and took refuge between the blankets, drowsy from the day. Zander's affection, his distraction, his protection...

Hours later, in the pitch blackness, I was shaken.

"Wake, Elaina." Hands shook again. A large hand gripped my shoulder.

I didn't know who it was, I began to scream as a hand clamped over my mouth. Did Carl come to take me away? Or did Callum fear?

"Calm yourself, my love, it is only me."

Zander. "What's wrong?" I leaned up on my elbow groggy from the depths of sleep.

He handed me my robe. "You need to come with me. Quickly."

"Is it Callum? Is he ill?"

He held a candle. "Callum is fine." Anxiety spilled from every feature.

I threw on my thick robe and slippers and followed him from the room. "Please, tell me." Worry surged.

He grabbed my hand. "We must hurry."

He led me down the hall and around the corner—past the paintings and past the hidden corner to the other bedrooms I'd not yet explored. What madness was this? *Bewitched*... I dashed the word away. I would know soon enough.

Doctor Rillian met us at the door farthest down the hall of this vast abbey. His look was grave. It seemed I was to meet the "body", the dangerous person I couldn't know of.

Zander stopped me, his lips drawing in a firm line. "I don't have time to explain. Forgive me." He opened the door to a large room with glowing candelabras, a form, thrashed upon the bed.

I stepped inside and saw the young man. My vision went black.

Chapter Twelve

My senses snapped to attention in a fury. Salts had been waved beneath my nose as Zander's arms held me fast. My eyes blinked in the flickering light. I flung myself away from him and to my knees at the edge of the bed. "*Matthew*."

Matthew. My nephew. Alive. His wounds were many. An arm was splinted, as were both legs, bound with strips of linen to sized straight planks. I took in the sight of him, the one that had drowned at sea. This was the body that Zander had carried within—and had kept from me.

"Matthew."

His eyes were open, but he didn't know me. He jerked back and forth, shuddering from fever.

Zander drew close and lay a hand on my shoulder. "I couldn't forgive myself if he…" He rubbed his eyes, "Dr. Rillian says we must pray. He may not last the night."

My heart broke. Must I grieve Matthew twice? Bury him twice? Why did Zander think him a danger to me? Never. Never, never. Matthew had been here these several days and Zander had withheld the truth from me. I'd been frivolously shopping in the village while this dear one lay at death's door.

I could have nursed him. Comforted him as I had when his own dear mother had died. He needed me—family. I faced Zander. "How could you? Why would you keep my own flesh from me?"

"I didn't want to."

I wasn't sure I believed him. I turned my attention back to Matthew. I stroked deep brown hair plastered to his forehead. His face bore terrible cuts and bruises. His lips—that often resembled Trevor's—were dry and chafed. Moments ago, I thought him gone forever. I dipped a cloth in water and swabbed away the sweat.

Dear, dear Matthew. Tears blurred my eyes. I croaked the question I hadn't wanted to ask. "How long does he have, Dr. Rillian?"

"He may linger several hours."

Hours. From death to life to death again. I prayed he would know I was with him until the last. That he would sense he wasn't alone—that I loved him deeply.

I continued to swab his brow and stroke his hair, repeating his precious name. Memories of our life together flooded my heart. I'd been a child when he was born. Was a wonder he ever learned to walk for the amount of time he spent clinging to my hip.

He'd been but a lad of six when he became motherless. Tears threatened to spill down my cheeks again. He'd been so confused. His mother had always been there for him and then one day, she disappeared. A swift illness had taken Julia and we'd all grieved deeply. I'd spent night after night with him curled up, crying himself to sleep.

Not long after, he and Trevor had moved back to Father's estate where our relationship solidified. My sweetest nephew. He'd grown into nearly a man before my eyes.

I blinked at the inconceivability. "A fourteen-year-old boy is *not* a threat to my life."

Zander grunted as he slipped to his knees and tried to keep his splinted arm from thrashing. "In this case, I feared you might inadvertently be a threat to his."

He wasn't making sense. I recalled the message I'd stumbled upon. And Zander's haste to depart almost as soon as we'd arrived.

"*Your inquiry and suspicion have proven correct. You know where to come for further contact. I must recommend swift removal...*"

"Where was he, before you brought him here? How did you know where to find him? Why didn't Carl find him and bring him home?" How on earth did his survival get overlooked? "Zander—*how*?"

Matthew mumbled. His eyes shuttered, his forehead searing hot.

I looked at Dr. Rillian. "Please—what can I do?"

The Doctor poured something in a vial and stepped towards her. "Pray, Lady Sherborne. Pray." He administered the medicine. "To help with his pain."

His poor, poor broken body. But Lord, that he might live! I prayed as I have never done before. "The Zephyr wrought its havoc upon you." He finally stilled and his breathing grew softer. The medicine calmed the tempest.

Zander handed me a cup of tea, but I wouldn't take it. "Elaina? His broken bones—the wreck didn't cause those indignities."

"I don't understand. The Zephyr was wrecked."

He shut his eyes and nodded. "He swam ashore and hid."

"Why?" *Oh, Matthew.*

"He didn't know who to trust. Your nephew has been very brave."

"How long have you known?"

"I merely suspected. His body hadn't been discovered and..." Zander caught my eyes with his, uncertain whether to tell me. "I hired runners but someone else got to him first."

"Who did this?"

Zander didn't answer, but gathered my hand in his and prayed. I then realized that there was only one reason I might be a threat to Matthew. And why Zander felt the need to keep his life and whereabouts a secret. Carl. Could it be? If I'd known and written to Aunt Honora or Lyvia of this miracle... What then?

It had mattered to Zander to keep us both safe. The letter from Trevor proved much—and yet proved that I only saw the tip of a mountain beneath the sea.

"You rescued him." Perhaps even from our own family.

"Only God can do so now."

If only Zander had confided in me—really knew he could trust me, I might have had more time with Matthew. Before he left me again.

"Believe me. I wanted to restore him to you."

"Was he lucid—when you carried him here that night."

He shook his head. "The doctor there gave him laudanum to make the journey. We placed him here. He came off the drug just as the fever set in."

"You spoke with him?"

"A little."

"Does he know I'm here? That we are married?"

Zander shook his head again. "My only goal was to get him to a safe place where he could heal. What little I've gleaned…"

"You hoped to learn something? About the wreck?"

"Yes."

I pressed a fist against my head. "And you thought we'd be a risk to each other."

"Yes. You are a risk." He gripped my hand tightly. "You must promise me not to tell anyone of his presence here. Tell no friends—no family—that he's been found."

I agreed. "It's all so strange."

"The brutality he's endured is inhumane." Zander's brows drew together. "He's only a boy."

"To survive such a tragedy only to be beaten so savagely." I caressed Matthew's fingers on his one unwounded hand. "I don't understand." I wept.

Zander tipped my head to lean on his shoulder and stroked my unbound hair. He sought to soothe what might never be undone. I leaned into his tenderness despite my frustration. No one had held me so since Mother died. Indeed, I had no one else to cling to.

"As angry as I am, I can't imagine Carl had any part in this." Yet I'd read Trevor's own mistrust. How deep did it go? Mistrust in expenditures? More? I grimaced. He'd been willing enough to put a price on me.

Matthew had gone very still, I feared the worst. Doctor Rillian checked his pulse, listened to his lungs. "He is still with us."

I felt little relief. As time passed, so would Matthew.

I groaned awake. No longer on the narrow bench, but on a cot. No doubt one that served Dr. Rillian these past several days. Morning had come. Zander stood, looking out of the window while the healer snored in a chair in a dark corner. I shifted my sight to Matthew and made my way back to his side.

Such a look of peace spread across his face, I worried that he'd flown while I slept. Zander rejoined me.

"There is still breath in him, Elaina."

I touched his head. Nothing. I felt around his face, his neck, and chest. "His fever is gone. It's gone!"

Zander lifted his wrist and checked his pulse. He gently set Matthew's arm down, and felt his head, wonder filling his face. "You're right." His eyes squeezed shut, was that a tear? "Thank you, God."

Matthew's eyes flickered open, his lips moved—he tried to wet them.

Zander handed me a cup. "Give him a spoonful of tea."

I did as told—had I not nursed him before?

"Auntie 'laina." His voice crackled.

"I'm here, Matthew."

His fingers moved to find mine. "Home."

"I'm here. With you." I leaned in. "You aren't dreaming."

His face squeezed. "Father..." he gulped. I fed him another spoon of tea. "Father didn't make it."

I smoothed his brow with my other hand. "I know, he is with Jesus."

"I couldn't come home."

Dr. Rillian woke and rushed to the other side of the bed. "Have we a morning miracle?" The man checked his pulse. "Strong. Good. You've been out of your mind for more than a sennight."

"Who are you?" He rasped. "Matthew's hand grew agitated.

"I am Dr. Rillian and you are Lord Sherborne's guest."

"Lord Sherborne?"

Zander moved into his line of sight. "Yes, Master Dawes." He pressed a hand to Matthew's shoulder. "You are safe now. I won't let anything else happen to you."

"My lord...I..." Tears began to stream. "I couldn't..." He shook his head.

"Steady yourself, young man, or I will have to see you back to sleep." Dr. Rillian looked over his spectacles. "Your Aunt is most anxious, you see."

Matthew nodded weakly. What couldn't he do?

"Where am I?"

I knelt by his side. "You are at Goodwyn Abbey, Lord Sherborne's estate."

"How?"

"He carried you here—away from those who would do you harm."

"I remember." He tugged my hand. "How'd you know to come?"

"My dear, Lord Sherborne and I are wed."

His eyes brightened and the corners of his mouth twitched. "Father told me he wanted to court you."

"Did he now?" Grief filled our eyes.

Matthew shifted, so we gently lifted him settling him against the pillows.

Fresh pots of tea and soup were delivered to the room. Molly avoided my gaze. Wasn't fair that she knew and I didn't—but I had to cast that thought away. Much wasn't fair. Even miracles. I fed him and once again saw the little boy he used to be. But for the cast of new whiskers on his face, I would think him still.

Doctor Rillian took the tray from my hands and pulled me aside. "Lady Sherborne, your nephew is in a great deal of pain. He's holding back, I think, because he doesn't want to worry you."

"What are you saying?"

"I think it best if you take your leave for a few hours so that he can freely feel his pain—and cry if need be."

"But he's always—we—" How could I explain how close we'd been?

"He is near a man. Let him his dignity." Dr. Rillian leaned closer and whispered. "We must wash him, change his garments, and reset his splints."

I loathed the thought of leaving his side. I kissed his forehead and Zander followed me. He took my hand within his hold and led me back to the bedroom I'd abandoned many hours before. "Get some sleep."

"Don't know if I can ever sleep again." I swallowed at a thought I'd been afraid to voice. "Don't tell me Trevor is also still alive? Should I check the remainder of the unused bedrooms?"

Hurt crossed his bloodshot eyes. I hadn't meant to sound so trite – or cutting.

"No, Elaina. Of course not." He brushed hair from my face and tucked it behind my ear.

Of course not. Exhaustion spoke for me.

He followed me through my door and closed it behind us. "Can I trust you not to write to your family?"

"No one at all?" I felt my lips tighten.

His jaw worked. "I suppose ending all communication isn't the right way to go about this."

"I can't pretend Aunt Honora doesn't exist."

His eyes landed on the letter I'd retrieved from his office. "You—"

I finished for him. "You read it."

His lips curved in a frown. "I thought you changed your mind."

Nausea roiled. "The letter was in bad taste." I moved to toss it into the fire, but Zander stopped me.

"If you don't mind, I find something of interest—"

"Naught but gossip." I handed the pages to him.

"And yet a thread of truth may be found." He stepped towards the door. "Get some sleep. We'll talk when you wake."

I'd been too sharp. "Zander—you saved Matthew's life."

He leaned against the door frame. "But I wasn't fast enough."

Matthew's broken body spoke of those with murderous intent. He most certainly would have died if Zander hadn't suspected his survival.

My emotions spun with exhaustion. "I didn't mean to be angry."

He shrugged. "I don't blame you."

"Please—don't bear this burden alone." He knew what I asked.

He pointed to my bed with his chin. "Sleep." He touched my hand and shut the door.

Chapter Thirteen

"Do you recall anything else?" Zander sat beside Matthew holding a black lead pencil and foolscap.

Matthew's brow wrinkled. "No—it's all a mite cloudy."

Heads turned at my entry.

Dressed in a fresh shirt with washed hair, Matthew sat up in bed. The late afternoon sun glowed within the room, directly onto Zander. He'd shaved though his eyes were still heavy. Handsome despite the lack of sleep.

"Auntie 'Laina." Matthew attempted a pitiful smile around the scabbing cuts. "I must have been dreaming. Is it true that you married him?"

In an answer, Zander rose, took my hand, and led me to Matthew's side. "Truly wed."

"If Father were here, he'd want to give you his blessing."

A lump rose in my throat. "I daresay he would."

"Since he isn't, I give you mine, Auntie. Lord Sherborne..." He lifted a shaky hand to touch ours. "I should have liked to been at the wedding." He grimaced as his hand lowered. "I am glad of it. Father told me that if anything were to happen," he licked his lips, "I should find Lord Sherborne. 'Trust him,' he said. Did he tell you the same, Auntie 'Laina?"

"He did, Matthew." In so many words. I eased into the chair at Matthew's side.

A smirk filled his face. "And you fell in love with him quickly, is that the way of it?"

"If you weren't incapacitated, I would tickle your ribs." I smiled and leaned in. "I still might."

He gasped a laugh. "Don't you dare." His lips drew downward in thought. "Uncle Carl—he—"

Zander drew close.

"He hurt Father." He shook his head. "I don't recall how—but I know he did. I remember flashes of his anger—and…" Confusion rose in his eyes. "Never seen him that way before." He searched my face. "Tell me the truth. Did he die with the others?"

"No. He survived."

Matthew cast his eyes to Zander.

Zander put a hand on my shoulder. "You are safe here. I promise that no more ill will befall you—either of you."

"Has ill befallen you, Auntie?"

"Yes. Thinking you gone from me." I swiped the corner of my eye. "Thank God you are alive. How could I get on without you, tell me that?"

Dr. Rillian arrived bearing another tray and a bundle of bandages. "My patient must rest now. Be good and get some fresh air. Both of you. Out of here. Doctor's orders."

We had no choice but to obey. Lord willing, Matthew would be on his feet again.

Less than an hour later, donned in my riding habit, a groomsman held Niveus by the bridle while Zander put his hands around my waist and guided me off the mounting block, strong arms lifting me atop the side saddle.

It had been years since my riding lessons, but the knowledge quickly returned.

"Hold your cane on the other side—here is the balancing strap. Good." Zander mounted Misty-eye and came beside me. "Adjusted? Ready for the reins?"

Niveus seemed gentle enough. "Yes." The groomsman handed them over.

"Not so tight, my lady. Nice and slack. Easy, she'll take to ye and learn your desires over time."

Zander spoke to the groomsman. "You may saddle Broonie and follow at a distance."

"Yes, my lord."

Callum stood with his hands on his hips, a wide smile spread across his face. " 'at Nivy's a sweetheart, she is. 'At one'll take love as it's given."

Niveus gave a nod.

Callum giggled. "See? She agrees."

Niveus shifted on her hooves and I tightened my grip on the saddle. Those two had a connection.

Zander smiled. "We'll go slowly. Timothy won't be far behind. We'll get off and walk if we need to."

Zander moved ahead. I pressed my stick against her side and she followed Misty-eye as though expecting a tour of the place.

The cold air made way for the sun's bright shine. Its gaze warmed us. Zander seemed at ease as he guided us atop one sloping hill, then another. The only sound, the stamping of hooves. We were together, but alone in the wide world.

Zander led us down another path, another slope looked over his tenant's cottages spread out across many fields. Smoke curled from the chimneys and children's laughter floated up from the valley. "I'll take you down another day."

"I look forward to it." I truly did.

We rode until the sun began to sink with bright hues of lavender and oranges, betwixt the hills, lingering until every last color had dissipated from the evening sky. Dr. Rillian proved right. Fresh air was exactly what we needed.

"What will we do, Zander?"

"Take each day as it comes." He spoke more to the views than to me. How much did we—did he really face?

"Now that Matthew is safe—"

Zander pulled Misty-eye around to face me. "I'm afraid the issue is far from over."

"Are there other innocents to be rescued?"

He took a breath and held his tongue—remained quiet as we rode back to the stables. Zander lifted me down and let Timothy and Callum care for the horses.

We went inside and changed from our habits before supper. Zander was quiet. Thoughtful.

"How long will it take for Matthew to heal?"

"Wish I knew. The fever took us by surprise."

He folded his arms and I stopped eating. "You've been under a great deal of strain. To add to your concerns seems unkind." He rubbed the back of his neck. "Do I cause more damage by keeping you ignorant of the situation? If I do make all known to you, will it cast darkness upon you?"

"It is so bad?" Indeed, what I'd seen portended such.

"It may well be."

"And by my knowing, you believe it may cast my soul into melancholy?"

"You are straightforward, Elaina."

"I despise pretenses. Constantly guessing at motives and designs. Too many years in society taught me much about falsity."

"My mother—as your aunt said—didn't handle the gossip well. Or a certain duke's manipulations. My father did what he could to keep the worst from her, but..."

"Gossip spreads its venom, regardless."

"Indeed."

"This is why you didn't return to Town?"

"I returned, my parents did not. At least, I did not return to society. Like you, I did not care to subject myself to its ambitious claws."

"Yet a baron like yourself may climb the societal heights, in any case." I echoed his friend, the vicar.

"I did not care for the view."

I was quickly coming to know that we were more alike than different. I should have enjoyed knowing his parents. "Did Lady Sherborne ever recover?"

"She had to learn whom she could trust—it was hard." His eyes captured mine.

I looked away. Yes, so very hard. Even now, after society had performed its worst upon us, another kind of evil flanked my awareness. This evil put my brother to death—and I didn't know who else. It loomed, inescapable. Society itself, regardless of rank, embodied equal amounts of potential and poison.

"I only wish Trevor had made me aware of his predicament before he left. I wonder why he didn't." Trevor often tried to stand in for Father, but would confide in me as a brother. "I take it Matthew didn't know of anything either?"

Zander tossed his napkin to the table. "Come, let us sit near the fire."

Ever the gentleman, he led me before the snapping flames and seated me, and took a chair opposite.

He cleared his throat. "As often as I've begged you to trust me, I understand that might take a while."

I thought of his conduct over the time that I'd known him and guilt thrashed my conscience. To think of who I might have been thrust upon—those who would have had no love for me but would have merely used me. I winced. This man was intent on taking me to his heart. Slowly, generously. He would not force himself upon me. Seemed, in truth, to despise the idea.

A tear slipped down my face. I did trust him. Or was learning to. Like the man who begged the Lord to help his unbelief, I needed constant assurance. Zander pressed his handkerchief into my hand and I wiped the tear away. "I'm tired of weeping."

"It's understandable. I am so very sorry for keeping Matthew from you. I had to be certain...I...had to be certain of you..."

Of course. I understood that now. I don't know how I would have acted in his position. I took a deep breath. "I do trust you." Another rogue tear followed the last. "I trust you more than anyone I've ever known—or ever thought I could trust." This was the truth. Since Trevor was gone—and my father, despite his inability to keep his pockets lined. I was entirely dependent on Zander.

He leaned forward, interest lighting his eyes. "It scares you a little?"

I shrugged. "I am inexperienced at being a wife."

"And I as a husband."

Would I ever stop blushing when he was near?

Zander poked the logs with an iron, the flames heightened. "About six months ago, Trevor found a stack of shipping manifests—or more accurately—pulled them from their hiding place at the office."

Seems he'd seen Carl checking a loose board in the corner, to the left of the desks. He didn't think anything of it. But then saw him do it again, that time, he replaced the board when he thought Trevor wasn't looking. When Carl left for an errand, he found the hiding place. He didn't expect to find what he had."

How strange. "An odd place to store shipping manifests, to be sure." I couldn't comprehend where this was going.

Zander shook his head. "Those manifests didn't belong to the Zephyr. They belonged to other companies. Duplicates had been made. Long lists of cargo, passengers, sailors, and their captains."

"I don't follow."

"Neither did Trevor, at first. He replaced them until he could make sense of it. When I arrived at the office, we were going to look over it together. That's the day you brought luncheon, do you recall?"

"Yes." He'd turned as though I'd startled him.

"But this time, the copies were gone, and in its place, a new stack. For different ships, including the Zephyr. With it was an alternate route—one that Dawes Shipping never used. Trevor immediately suspected foul play.

"When I did some digging, I found that only one of the ships listed had wrecked along the Cornish coast. The others had found safe passage and ensured delivery of their goods."

Zander continued. "Trevor felt badly for suspecting Carl had anything to do with a crime. Wrecks along Cornwall happen from time to time. Perhaps he was trying to remain organized. Being one's own secretary required careful counting and recording. But still, why the duplicate copies? And why hide them?"

I placed my hand upon my head as though to will my understanding.

"The Zephyr was set to sail. He and I looked into the hiding place one last time, if only to sweep away our convictions. Found the Zephyr's manifest—half completed—, but this time, including coordinates for routes heretofore unconsidered. One specific route had been marked with a star. At that point, we knew he had to be planning something. But to wreck one's own ship? This we did not comprehend. Worried, Trevor talked to the Zephyr's captain, who assured him that all was well.

We were going to confront Carl, when we learned that he'd decided to board the ship and travel with the goods. It made sense to have Trevor go to observe and make certain that the business functioned as it was supposed. His dark premonition increased as their cast-off date neared..."

Zander stared into the fire—reliving those days?

"I had a bad feeling too, yet I encouraged him. If he found Carl in some mischief, we might be able to correct his course. If there was no substance to our fears, we might rest easy.

Bear in mind, Elaina, I was not privy to the nature of your brother's ledgers. Had I been..." He took a deep breath. "Trevor wrote his observations to me daily, and the letter that you recently read. He felt something was about to happen, and still, I counseled him to board the Zephyr—keep eyes on his brother's business. So you see, my regrets are profound."

"You could not know." Nor Trevor. Carl wouldn't have taken Matthew along if he thought their lives were in danger. Likely their debts would have drowned them regardless.

"As an investor of rank, and a friend, Trevor listened to me. Had I listened to my own sense of unease, I would have withdrawn the lad. Stopped the journey. And no one would have died. Not a single passenger or sailor."

A log shifted in the coals. "Unease can trick the mind."

"In this case, it was truth, not a trick."

Zander must not take this blame. "Trevor was a grown man who made his own decisions. I know that once he set his mind to it, he wouldn't be put off." And in some sovereign, mysterious plan, God did not prevent it. The reasons eluded me despite how intently I wondered.

"Do you think Carl wrecked his own ship? Doesn't make sense."

Zander shook his head. "No. It doesn't. I am not certain he did."

"And why beat a survivor—or—"

Zander joined my musing. "Or why won't Matthew tell me what his father and uncle were fighting about aboard the ship that day..." He stood. "Whatever Carl was doing, it was his undoing. And might be ours as well. Matthew is being tracked. I must know why to keep him safe."

"The other day, when you spoke to Mr. Thomhow—"

"Yes. I must appear to search for what I've already found. I've instructed the runners to continue "looking" for Matthew."

I pressed a hand to my heart." "Oh, Zander." Such a weight to carry.

"Now you know." He pulled a thread from his waistcoat and tossed it into the fire. "Nothing more may come of this. It is possible that Matthew was in the wrong place at the wrong time, that he was not specifically targeted, but..."

"You don't think so?"

"Dr. Rillian believes his injuries akin to torture. Premeditated."

The thought of Matthew enduring so much—I couldn't bear it. I drew fists to my eyes and wiped away angry tears.

"Elaina." Zander's hand was on my arm, but still the tears came, unstoppable.

"Elaina, I'm sorry. I'm so sorry." He pulled me to my feet. "Please, don't think of it."

"I am so angry, I—"

"Put it from your mind. Please." His lips softly caressed where my tears had been. He kissed me. My eyes, my cheeks, my temples—until his lips found mine. Warm and sweet like wine, his love calmed the tempest of my sorrow. He pressed a kiss to my forehead and held me to his chest.

I found my voice again. "Thank you for trusting me."

"I'll also trust that you get a full night's sleep? It's been a long day." He released his hold and backed away. His expression full of care.

"It has." His embrace broken, a cold space grew between us.

When I came to breakfast in the morning, Zander was nowhere to be found.

I was becoming accustomed to the pattern.

Chapter Fourteen

My mind and dreams were filled with Zander. From his active interest in protecting Matthew—to his tenderness, and dare I say love? To wake and find him departed from Goodwyn stung. All I wanted was to know what was coming next.

I spent the day with Matthew, reading to him as I had when he was much younger. Dr. Rillian told me that despite his bravado, he was still in much pain.

"How is it that you are able to be both nurse and doctor? I imagine Butterton has far-reaching needs."

"The village has its own physicians, my dear. I am retired, as much as doctors can retire, and have been serving Lord Sherborne these few years. There are tenants enough on his land to keep me busy."

"Where do you live?"

"Of the last few weeks? In this room. On the regular? In the cottage not far from the gatehouse."

"No wonder you always seemed to be at beck and call."

He bowed. "Always at your service, Lady Sherborne. And the lord's as well."

"Thank you for helping him."

"He's a braw lad."

"Will his legs…"

"I have the best hope." His eyes twinkled. "Tis a wonder how God can make the bone heal itself. If left out of alignment—well—the bone would grow back together the wrong way and the legs wouldn't match. The splints tell the bones which way to grow…protects them. All we need to do is keep them in place and be patient."

His words were meant to inform me of more than Matthew's condition. Mayhap my own.

Dr. Rillian sent a knowing glance over his bound legs and arms. "Will be many months before he is fully right again."

Months…I looked at Matthew sleeping—the medicines the doctor gave him helped with his pain but took his company. Some color had come back to his face, this was a relief. I would pay a visit to Mrs. Thomhow and meet the children.

I collected my shawl and walked to the gatehouse. The cheerful woman was overjoyed to have my visit. Her red-headed darlings spent the hour impressing me with a variety of impromptu antics. We were in the middle of a game when Mr. Thomhow entered the room, his ever-present satchel around his shoulder.

"I hate to interrupt, but might I have a word?" He stood and I followed him through the doorway.

The door closed behind us as Mr. Thomhow settled his satchel on his desk and rifled within. "I am remiss, sorry to say. My morning duties scattered me about the place, I quite forgot to have this message sent up to you."

He handed me a folded square.

"Do forgive me, my lady. Won't happen again."

"From my Zander?"

"Yes, Lady Sherborne."

My stomach flip-flopped. He hadn't left without word after all. "I thank you." My smile could not be suppressed.

Mrs. Thomhow poured tea, then I bundled my cloak and took my leave. Halfway back to Goodwyn, I leaned against an ancient oak and read his message.

My love,

I must see to things in London, check into some details that may or may not have bearing on our discussion. I will return as soon as able. How is it that I miss you already, though I've not yet left? You are becoming more and more dear to me, my wife.

I am yours,

Zander

I'd recently resigned myself to spinsterhood, or the thoughts of it. Marriage seemed unlikely and out of reach. So caught up in the romance of his words, the memory of his kiss, that I didn't notice the lack of a forwarding address until later. He'd only be gone a few days, I supposed. Hoped…

That night, Molly shook me awake. "Dr. Rillian says to fetch you. Sorry, my lady. He's that upset."

Entering Matthew's room, I saw Dr. Rillian holding down a leg and arm. He thrashed, much like he had before. "Is the fever back?"

"No. The medicine can confuse the mind. He's having a nightmare. I've tried to wake him, but..." He shook his head. "He can't come out of it."

I took my place by his side, his hand in mine, I stroked his hair. The poor thing was trapped in a place of terror. "Matthew. I'm here. Come back to me."

"No, no, no." His face screwed up with pain. "Don't hurt me, no..." His whole body spoke to the cruelty he was suffering.

He relived his torture.

I reached past my own grief, past our memories together and sang a song. One I used to sing him to sleep. My little nephew. I lay my head on his pillow and sang it over and over, low in his ear until he stopped and blinked awake.

"They were going to hurt me again, Auntie."

"I'm here, Matthew. You are safe."

"What if they find me?" Terror clung like sweat.

"Do they want to find you, dear? Why should they?"

He blinked, his lips moving, his eyes darting about the room. "I don't have it."

I had to know. "What don't you have?"

"Uncle Carl thought—" he shook his head. "I don't have it."

"Did Uncle Carl think you had something?" My gut twisted.

"He didn't know—it fell when they fought. I found it and then the ship—" A flood of tears. "There wasn't time. Father—he pushed me up from the cabin. The storm—the rocks—then..." He squeezed his eyes. "I couldn't breathe. I swam but I couldn't breathe."

The memory was causing him anguish. "That's enough. Stop talking. Breathe now, Matthew."

"I'm trying." Anxiety clawed at him.

I sang the same song again, this time Matthew kept his sea-green eyes on me, blinking slowly until his lids became heavy with sleep and calm. I prayed peace over his writhing spirit.

Dr. Rillian pressed his hands together and bowed his thanks. He whispered, "I will send for you if he becomes restless again. Thank you, dear."

I took his proffered chamberstick and made my way to my room, to the desk. I took out some writing paper and recorded everything Matthew said. He had something important to care for, but didn't have it anymore...What did it mean?

Chapter Fifteen

For three more days, I waited. Matthew still struggled. I sang him to sleep each night, whether he desired it or no. And like a baby, he succumbed to my voice. He didn't speak of his memories though he did relive his beating a few more times. Dr. Rillian wasn't surprised.

"The young soldier is too tender of bearing to suffer such—any man might be. Were he a few years older and hardened by battle…well…" Dr. Rillian thought better of his words. I realized it was because I am Lady Sherborne, of a delicate gender and class. I wanted to know what soldiers suffered and asked him bluntly.

"Some do better than others, my lady."

"You served?" That made sense. Most men did.

"Aye. Earned my spurs in the colonies." His eye twitched. "Long time ago."

"Will he learn to move past his fears?"

Dr. Rillian shoved his spectacles up. "He must learn to fight. Defend himself."

"Perhaps he will not need such training now that he is safe."

"Forgive me, my lady, you asked how he might move past his fears? I told you. *Scientia sit potentia*. Knowledge is power. He must learn, on this I cannot be moved."

A deep voice interrupted. "Dr. Rillian is right."

"Zander! You are home."

His lips lifted in a half a smile. Whiskers shadowed his face. He held out his hand to me. "Come."

We walked down the hall as Zander removed his coat. "I rather like courting you, but it proves quite a challenge."

"Oh, really?" How hard would he try?

"If we were in London, I would invite you to the opera. Or to Gunters."

"Gunters—it is too cold for an ice." I shivered.

"You are right. Bad idea." He opened our parlor door. "I might call with flowers in hand."

"This you may do." My heart thumped at his nearness. "Where are they?"

"Alas, I have no flowers."

"Callum seems to manage well enough."

"Hmmm." He closed the door and folded his arms. "We are quickly running out of options." He shrugged. "I suppose I might kiss you again..."

I gulped. "Or go riding..."

"Riding?" He drew closer with a grin. "Too cold."

The wind howled in response, rattling the windows, sending groans down the chimney.

I cleared my throat. "I'm not sure courting couples should kiss at all, I mean—"

A wrinkle appeared between his brows. "Do they not?"

"Not without immediate ramifications. If they are caught."

"Marry—or else?"

"Pretty much…I suppose a courting couple ought not be caught alone."

"We are very much alone. Have been many times now."

"It seems we are fated, my lord."

He leaned in and brushed his lips against mine. "Since the beginning of time, my dear." He pulled away.

"I didn't realize that Lord Sherborne was such a flirt, the like I have never seen."

"Only in regards to his wife—never has he been before now." He pressed another kiss to the side of my lips.

"Truthfully?"

"Mmm." His hands went to his hips. "Too busy thwarting coquettes and their wily schemes. Could scarcely spot a genuine woman among them." His eyes crinkled with humor. "I do recall a certain young beauty who used to drink in the flirtations as though she enjoyed them on the regular."

His words stung. "They weren't real." Not a single flirtation or attraction held value. I'd discounted them long ago.

"You are correct. Mine, however, are very much…" He kissed the other side of my lips. "True."

My heart sped.

"I think it would befit every man to court his wife. On a daily basis." He winked. "Join me in my study? I don't fancy leaving your presence."

"Scandalous."

His eyes darkened as he disappeared through his bedroom door. "Careful, dear."

I stared after him like a besotted female which I suppose I was.

Losh, I'd been utterly distracted. For good reasons. I rushed to my desk and pulled out the notes I'd made and joined my husband in the study. My husband...the more I said it, thought it, the more real it became.

I took the chair by the fire as he and Mr. Thomhow spent a half hour going over accounts and expenditures. I ought to have taken out my needlework, but holding such information, my work would likely have had to be restitched. Instead, I listened and waited for my chance alone with Zander.

Mr. Thomhow set letters on the desk. "These came, I saw fit to open them."

I wondered if any were from Carl.

"I realize you've just returned." Mr. Thomhow sent me a glance, then back to Zander. "But I would advise going immediately. Read the letters and let me know your decision." He turned and bowed to me. "Lady Sherborne."

I waited for the door to shut before approaching his desk. "While you were gone, Matthew had nightmares. When he woke he said some things that might be important. I wrote them down for you—"

He took the papers and went over each line. "He found something? Did he not say what it was?"

"No. I did ask, but he was reluctant to speak of it again."

"And he says he doesn't have this object any longer?"

"I assume that is what he meant to say. Had he any belongings?"

"Your nephew didn't have a stitch on his back other than what the fisher wife gave him."

"Did she find him?"

"Her husband. The boy had been set adrift in a boat, unconscious and as you see him." He tapped his fingers on the desk. "The runners had lost his scent until then."

"You were waiting for word during our wedding. He was why we had to rush away. I suppose you are having Carl followed."

He cocked his head, a slight smile touching his lips. "You are a shrewd one."

"Is that how you intercepted the letter—about me?"

"That despicable note was being bandied about the gentleman's club. I'd gone that night by invitation." He seemed slightly embarrassed.

"Trevor must not have told Carl about your…interest…"

He jerked a nod. "Or he would have used you as leverage and exacted a higher price. Disregard it." He captured my eyes. "You, however, are priceless. No doubt about that." He set my notes aside and reopened a ledger. "When Matthew wakes, we'll see if he is ready to talk. Pray that he does, Elaina."

I resettled by the fire with neither book nor occupation to keep me busy but prayed as I have never done before.

A few hours later, we sat by Matthew's bedside and sought for the truth.

"I didn't steal it." He shook his head. "Uncle Carl dropped it—they fought."

"Dropped what?"

"A bag of something. Didn't know what it was until the next day. When the ship hit the rocks, I stuffed it in my pocket. The water and fire—it—" he took a deep breath.

"The men who beat you, did they require it?" Zander asked.

"Uncle Carl—when we were hit, he shouted at me to guard it with my life."

"And so you did. Nearly died for it, young man."

"I didn't know I would, my lord. They asked for it once—and then…" He grimaced.

"Did you know them by sight?"

"No. Never saw them before in my life."

I wondered, "How did they know to ask you, of all people?"

Zander tapped his chin. "I wonder the same. How did they know to approach you?"

Matthew's head bent down. "I went looking for Uncle Carl. In case he survived."

"After hiding in the caves?"

He nodded.

"And did you bury—"

Finally, he shared the truth. "It was a set of keys, my lord." He panicked. "I don't know what they belong to. I swear it!"

"No need to swear, I believe you. Can you tell me which cave you hid them in?"

Matthew bit his lip, trying ever so hard not to cry. A tell he'd not overcome since infancy. "What do they unlock?"

"No idea. But if those men were willing to beat you and leave you for dead, then the keys must open something significant."

"After I hid them, I kept myself scarce. The wreckers knew what they were about. Took everything. Even searched the bodies."

I shivered. Such evil amid desperation.

"Lord Sherborne, I will draw a map." His fist clenched. "But promise me you'll be safe."

Zander put his hand upon his arm. "You have my word."

We left him with assurances. Zander was anxious but pasted on a smile. "We dine at Butterton Hall this eve. Did you remember?"

"Then it's a good thing my evening dresses are ready." I knew he was going to leave again, to chase this elusive enemy. Was it Carl—or someone else? Please not my own brother.

"When do you leave?"

"First thing in the morning." His eyes held a question. "Come with me."

"Leave Matthew?"

"He will be in Dr. Rillian's care."

"He will worry if I go."

"You will be in no danger." He took my hand, bowed over it and kissed the ring. "I've placed guardians about the town."

"You'll be able to look for the keys more easily if I go..." One step closer to ending the mayhem. I hoped.

"We can appear to be on our honeymoon," I suggested.

"Appear?"

I smiled. "We are still courting, are we not?"

"Mm. Of course."

"Perhaps we are past courting, Elaina. I might propose. Put a ring on your finger..."

"My finger is filled, as you can see."

"Tell me it isn't hopeless? Because..." He slipped a golden circlet from his waistcoat and knelt on one knee. "Will you marry me, Elaina?"

Molly, wide-eyed, sped past us and around the corner. I stifled a giggle.

"I've confused the maid. What gossip might ensue within these very walls? Please say yes and quickly."

"I suppose if I must I must."

He took my right hand instead and slipped the ring on the empty fourth finger, sealing it with another kiss. I would never be able to look at these rings and see anything else but his love for me.

He pulled me into the parlor from the hall. "I suppose engaged couples may kiss?" He didn't wait for an answer. His hands slipped around my waist, his lips found mine, softly, gently, lingering.

He lifted his head. "I was terrified that you would find me disagreeable."

"You are not the usual baron."

"You find normal barons disagreeable?"

"Unless they are like you. Exactly like you." I bit my lip. "I don't need to find out."

"I am relieved." His hand lifted my eyes to his, his breath a whisper. "I will never force you to my chambers."

I swallowed, looking for words—anything. Zander had given me every hope for love and goodness in our future. "God-willing, we will have children someday."

He repeated my words as though sealing a solemn promise. "Indeed. God-willing, we will have children someday."

The clock tolled. Dinner at Butterton Hall…We must hasten.

He winked. "How fast can you be ready?"

Chapter Sixteen

Between Zander's lips and curiosity about the keys, I could scarcely concentrate on the offerings at this lavish dinner party.

Lady Camden had withheld no expense. Her nimble digging into my parentage had not surprised. What little she unearthed hopefully gave her no links whatsoever to her memories. It had been over ten years since she'd been to Town. Before tonight, we were utter strangers.

Being a wife to a baron put me at a higher rank, or she might have pressed further than manners dictated. I was glad that she held her questions in for I did not want to answer them. Reaching higher, as the vicar put it, proved difficult even with the best of intentions.

Her youthful nieces, however, queried at every turn. Their time in London would come the following year with hopes for romance and marriage. I had been exactly the same, dreaming of my knight in shining armor. What little they knew of real romance—what a stark comparison to the love growing in my heart.

My eyes wandered to Zander again, sitting across the room engaging Lord Camden in discussion. I'd begun to understand his expressions. He wasn't happy. The line between his brows deepened despite his polite smile.

One of the girls leaned into my ear. "Tell us how it's done. How exactly did you catch a baron?"

By the grace of God, who looks not to titles, but to the man within... "Pray for him. Ask God to send you the husband you are meant to have."

The silly child giggled. "I shall pray for a duke in that case." Her sister rejoined, "Why not a prince?"

Lady Camden came to my rescue. "Music, girls. Play the duet you've been practicing." The two skittered away.

The vicar was in attendance, much to my delight. He escorted me to a chair and joined me. "I heard your answer." He grinned.

"I'm afraid they mistook my meaning."

"Even so, you planted a seed. If the girls cast their sights on God first, she could come to know the holiness of unions."

"I hope so. Was a lesson hard-learned." I'd entered my own holy union, as the vicar put it, in a state of shock and a sense of duty. At the time, I could think no further than my grief about my brother's death and failures. I had prayed, to be sure, despite the strong nudging from Carl and Aunt Honora to accept him. Sometimes answers can be limited by options.

"You are in love with him." The vicar's deep voice broke into my thoughts. He laughed at my gaping, wordless reply. "Don't mind me, dear, though I am glad of it. Lord Sherborne has been praying for you these many months. It's answered prayer that the one who has been on his heart also has stolen it."

I tried to keep my blush at bay. "Reverend, why is it you are not married?" His responding guffaw filled the room, causing the girls to stop mid-playing. "Such presumption. Would you believe it? My own wedding is in a month."

Even at his age? Good for him. "My congratulations." I joined his laughter. "I look forward to making her acquaintance."

"As she looks forward to making yours." He winked.

Zander came to my side and together we paid our parting respects to the guests and family.

In the coach, on the way back to Goodwyn, Zander brooded. "Lord Camden invited me to place a bet." His anger swelled. "On shipping companies."

"Zander?"

"As though it were a horserace. How insipid."

I spent the rest of the evening packing my trunk. Tomorrow, I would join Zander on this undercover quest. I hated leaving Matthew. What if he took a turn for the worse? I'd begged Zander to know the gritty details, and he'd told me. I was as entwined with this situation as I was in the Dawes family.

Whatever we found, I hoped Carl proved innocent. I prayed that his bargaining my life had been nothing more than a desperate move. I hoped that whatever his secrets, Carl was innocent of crime, and that Lyvia and the children were safe. Yet, if he had orchestrated a shipwreck, the lives of more than thirty were on his hands. How could he bear such guilt? How could anyone?

We boarded the coach as a thick fog had settled around Goodwyn. The air had turned colder, the freeze of winter brisked about the corner of autumn with icy tendrils. Zander handed me in and settled my feet upon a coal-filled foot warmer and covered me in thick fur.

"We will be curious tourists indeed, visiting Cornwall in this weather." I shivered.

Zander grinned. "One glance from you will keep me warm."

"A glance will do? Not a kiss?" I should not have tempted him.

"Did I say a glance only? Surely, I meant a kiss." He pressed his lips to my cheek.

"Do you say more, you will shock the footman."

"I daresay he will recover." He settled next to me, venturing beneath the fur, our feet touching.

The long ride to Cornwall will be forever sealed in my memory. We spent the hours listening. I heard his inmost thoughts and hopes, and he listened to mine. In no way did I feel my desires exposed to ridicule, but rather cared for, and nurtured. Sharing my heart so openly had been a risk. But I'd found that the rewards had been great.

He held me with his arm about my shoulders. Did he feel the wonder that I did? This was a depth of love I didn't know existed.

"Have I asked you to marry me yet?"

"Twice, my lord."

He reached his left hand across his lap to hold mine.

We arrived to the village. I saw the sea, curving around the land. Vast and endless. A grave to many. We exited the carriage as the cutting wind blew against our faces bringing with it the low growl of the ocean, a dirge of woes. I hadn't thought that I would face the self-same ocean that carried Trevor away from us and nearly killed Matthew.

The granite stone inn stood narrow and high in a crowded row of businesses and homes. The sky had darkened, letting the glow of lanterns shine into this cold place.

Zander led me inside the inn and we were ushered into a private parlor where he instructed the proprietor as to our needs. "Yer rooms be ready in a blink, my lord. M'lady." The man bowed and left to retrieve our supper of simmering stew and bread.

We ate at the small table by the fire as sounds of the tavern filtered through. A jumble of deep voices, the scent of ale, a rare laugh.

"It is colder than I thought it would be." Zander looked at me in concern. "But it can't be helped. We need to find Matthew's keys."

"Yes." I couldn't wait for a proper cup of strong tea.

The door opened. "Right this way, my lord."

We traveled up the narrow stair to a door at the other end of the hall. "Just as you asked, m'lord. The largest room we have. Ring if you need anything, anything at all." His smile was overbroad.

"Thank you."

Candles had been lit within the single, large chamber. A good-sized desk, a wing chair, seaside facing windows, one bed. *Oh...*

Zander cleared his throat and pointed. "That couldn't be helped either. But look underneath." A trundle cot hid beneath, intended for a lady's maid or a footman. "I will take the cot, of course."

"Are you sure? Will you fit?" His legs would dangle from the end. "No indeed. I will take it instead."

He jerked his head side to side. "No. In this case, you will obey as you vowed at the altar and take the bed."

I dared a smile. "We'll see about that."

He raised a brow. "Are we about to have our first argument?"

"Are we? I hope it will be over soon..."

Our trunks were delivered along with a blessed pot of tea. After drinking our fill, Zander set about observing Matthew's map. I prayed it was accurate and that we would find it quickly and return to him.

"Lord willing, the winds will die down tomorrow and we start exploring. It's getting late."

I thought about reading the book I'd brought but knew I couldn't keep my eyes open. I slipped behind the privacy screen and donned my night dress and robe. I eyed the trundle. I would quietly get within it, perhaps he wouldn't notice. He shouldn't have to fit his tall form on such a short bed. I would be perfectly comfortable—however foreign it felt to be in the same room with him, preparing for sleep.

He was engrossed in some newspapers from London. Making notes, reading. I blew out my candle and quietly slipped into the trundle. Still, he didn't turn to look at me. Good. I'd won our first argument.

I pulled the covers over my shoulder and watched him work in the weakly lit room for what seemed an hour. My eyes grew heavier. He folded the newspapers and bent his head into his hands. "Dear God," he whispered. "If only I'd listened. Too many."

He rested his chin upon his fist then leaned back in his chair. Would he come to bed at all? He got to his feet and stretched, and still he did not see me. I nearly held my breath. He reached into his satchel that hung on a peg and pulled out something long and wooden, bedecked with polished silver glinting in the light.

He sat down again and began to polish and clean the firearm, inside and out. I'd seen a flintlock pistol once—in Carl's hands the night before he sailed on the Zephyr.

A chill moved up my spine at the thought of its use. Or was it from the cold? Fire dissolved into low coals. We hadn't been provided with more wood. Zander said we would be safe. But were we? Who might be lurking nearby? Zander put the pistol back inside the satchel and turned to look at me upon the bed. I shut my eyes and pretended to be asleep.

A soft groan of regret escaped his lips. This way, we'd both get enough sleep. If only I might calm my anxious heart.

I heard him get ready for bed and the creak of the ropes when he crept within. He blew out his candle and I opened my eyes.

An hour went by. And two. I was cold. Too cold. I shifted on my side, trying to snuggle into my own warmth. Hopeless. I couldn't stop shivering. Is that how Matthew had felt, swimming in the freezing waves? Lord, Lord. That his suffering might end. I took a deep breath and ducked beneath my mountain of blankets. Even while in the depths of a London winter, I'd never been this cold. I feared I might grow ill.

Zander moved and I stilled. He got out of bed and knelt by the trundle. "You are freezing, Elaina." He slipped his arms beneath me, blankets and all and carried me to the place where he'd been lying. His warmth enveloped me, I could have cried with relief. And thanks. "I cannot let you suffer." He covered me with more blankets and slid in beside me, pulled my head to his chest, the length of him pressed against me. Blessed, blessed warmth. *For this grace, Lord, I thank thee...* Soon, I grew drowsy until the dim sun spilled through the windows.

I awoke with his arm still wrapped around me. I shifted and dared to see if he still slept. He blinked at me and smiled. "Warm enough?"

"Yes." I couldn't help grinning. "I am confounded by your kindness."

"Why?"

I couldn't answer for the lump in my throat and the tear in my eye. I'd determined not to weep again. No, I'd hold it back.

His hand came up and brushed the rogue drops away. "I am no kinder than you."

Wasn't true. Not even close.

"Once, I saw you gather a little girl in your arms. She as cold, clothed only in rags. You wrapped your shawl about her and held her until she was warm."

"How do you know this?" The child had gone looking for a doctor for her mother and had gotten lost.

"I saw you from the Dawes Shipping windows."

That was a year ago.

I bit my lip and looked at him with as much seriousness as I could muster. "What kindness might I do for you, Zander? I am at a loss. I feel as though I've been a...leech." I grimaced at my word choice.

"My loveliest fiancé and wife," He kissed my forehead. "Can you move to the pillow? I would hold you forever, but my arm has been numb this past hour." He laughed.

"Oh my." I shifted away.

He groaned as he lay back and rubbed his arm.

"I am so very sorry."

"I'm not. I rather liked holding you in my arms the night through." He winked. "Can we put aside the idea that you are beholden to me? We don't need obligations between us. Only openness. I beg you."

He was right.

A knock sounded at the door.

"That will be the footman with our tea." He swung from the bed. "Stay there, I'll get it." He still wore his shirt and trousers, now rumpled from the night.

The door shut behind him and he set the tray on the desk, poured a cup, and much to my surprise, brought it to me. My brothers couldn't pour tea for spilling over the table. "I'll go see about some firewood—we will not spend another freezing night as the last."

He left the room as I sipped the brew. So good, I crawled from the bed to get more. As I began to pour, a list caught my eye. Names in a long column. Check marks beside a few. Some crossed out. Mine topped the list—Elaina Dawes—with a line straight through it.

Was I meant to see this? Whatever did it mean?

Chapter Seventeen

Mine. Aunt Honora's. Carl. Lyvia—their children. Lines through all of the Dawes. Other names were listed, some with check marks beside them. Ones I didn't recognize but for one surname. Smith. Common enough.

How strange to see our names crossed out. By Zander's hand? Must be. He'd sat for hours last night reading the newspapers...head in hands. Discouraged. I looked back at the Dawes names and the truth rose to the surface. Trevor and Matthew's names weren't listed. Only those who survived the wreck.

This was a list of families.

Hands pulled the paper away. I hadn't heard him return. "Too many. Far too many people were affected by the deaths."

I turned and looked up at him as he scanned the names again. Until now, I'd only thought of how the Dawes family suffered. I hadn't thought of the far-reaching impact.

Zander took a deep breath as he tapped the list. "I can only do so much, but..."

The depth of his responsibility for the Zephyr's demise was evident. "It wasn't your fault."

He poured himself a cup of tea and swallowed. "I should have listened to Trevor. Stopped him from going. Pulled him back before it was too late."

"You couldn't have known." I peeked at the light grey sky. "The criminals are out there. Guilty of both death and plunder. And you aren't one of them." But Carl might be.

Zander set his cup down. "You're right. If I had the chance to repeat it, I would make the same decision. Repeat my encouragements to Trevor to observe the doings on the Zephyr." He shook his head. "I don't know. I've turned it around and around in my mind. Too late to change anything. No matter how much I wish to." He picked up the paper again. "But I can do something now."

"You would still carry the guilt upon your own shoulders? How?"

"By seeing to their needs. Compensating them for their loss." His lips drew a grim line. The weight he carried didn't belong to him.

"How will you go about it?"

"Runners. Village vicars. They report back to me on the families. If they are secure and well-fed," he pointed to check marks, "then I do not trouble them. If they appear to struggle, an anonymous gift is made. Or attempted." He pointed to one name with a star beside it. "This one refused. Too much pride to take a handout. At one level I understand. Money cannot bring back a loved one."

"I see." I poured another cup of tea. "You lost a significant amount, I shouldn't wonder."

"Yes. But that loss in no way compares to the forfeiture of a life."

"No, indeed." I touched his arm. "One way to help is to give the gift to the children. They may not accept from your hands, but indirectly sometimes works. For instance, the Parson is overburdened with oranges at Christmas and they're at risk of going to waste. Perhaps a child may be given a book at school…"

"I like the way you think." He bent to kiss me but paused at a knock at the door. Zander answered it. "Firewood. At last…no, I will build it myself. Thank you."

He carried the load like a laborer and set about warming our room. My heart was aflame. Could he see how he moved me? I drew near the fire as he tossed the last log on. He brushed off his hands. "I was interrupted." His look was focused.

"Were you?"

"Rudely." His brows knit together as he leaned in.

I shrugged. "It is rather nice to have a fire."

"It is rather nice to have a wife. My wife."

His hand came back to my jaw. I would never tire of his tenderness. "Zander, you aren't guilty. But you *are* good—" He quieted my argument with his lips, more intent than they'd ever been before—warmer, intoxicating…

He lifted his head. "Elaina. My Elaina. I don't know how good I am, but I do know that God certainly is. For Him to give you to me despite everything…" He shook his head. "His mercy is great. Boundless." He stroked my cheek with his thumb. "You are the sweetest, Love."

I rose to my toes and kissed his bristly cheek. "I only wished I could have known you sooner."

"For such a time as this, my love."

My jaw dropped. "What did you say?" Aunt Honora's words came back to me from our wedding day. Those of Queen Esther from my husband.

"I also wished to know you sooner. If not for Trevor's findings things might have been different. Honestly, my circumstances would be entirely depressing if it weren't for you, Elaina. I am thankful for you. More than you can know." Zander moved to the window. "I guess we ought to get on with it."

Our curious honeymoon tour of the shipwreck coast...

Zander stiffened. "What is he doing here?"

"Who?"

His brows rose. "The Duke of Banbury. Ridiculous notion."

"Do you need to be certain?"

Zander rifled through his trunk for a fresh set of clothes. "Aye." He dressed behind the screen and came out with his waistcoat wide open. "Too many buttons. Help me? I imagine you are more nimble of finger."

How could I resist him? His closeness never failed to warm me but I managed the row of ivory quickly—watched him tie his cravat, put on his jacket, and then, slide the pistol into his overcoat pocket.

"Zander—"

"I'll be right back. I promise." A kiss on my cheek and he was gone.

I quickly dressed myself before a maid was sent to tidy our room. I spent the hour impatiently waiting. How silly that I should feel half myself when Zander left the room. Did he feel the same? Is this what marriage did to those who loved? The vicar had called us "one". I was beginning to believe it.

When he returned, he seemed put out. "It was Banbury."

"Did you greet him?"

"I did not."

"You are acquainted though?"

"I wish that we were not. He is the one who caused my family's—my mother's—great distress."

"Oh…" The nasty rumors. I cringed. Was he the one "close to the throne" referenced by Aunt Honora?

"I suppose we should stay out of his sight, then?"

"Indubitably."

"This isn't the kind of village that draws a duke." Or a baron, for that matter.

Zander pulled Matthew's map from his satchel and tucked it inside his coat. "Cold or not, shall we attempt our hunt? As much as I've enjoyed our night here, I think we ought to be gone. Now."

He was concerned. He peered from the window. I donned my cloak, hat, and gloves, praying hopefully that we'd find the keys within the hour and be on our way.

Chapter Eighteen

Unforgiving. The rocks that jutted and sloped sent warning in the day, served to subvert explorers by night. The curve of the land bespoke safe harbor, the rocks certain demise. The one who held the lantern and worked the deception—who was it? I looked to and fro. The man mending fishing nets? The woman pushing the wheelbarrow? Anger surged at the thought of those who gave more value to greed than to life itself.

But isn't this the whole of history? A cycle of greed and grief going round and round? Zander's gifts could be like a stick in a wheel, changing the outcome. An offering that pointed to the ultimate kindness. An action that might change one's entire course. As mine did. I breathed in the brisk sea air and exhaled my anger. I must not be overtaken by its poison.

Zander pointed. "There."

He held my shoulders as I faced the rocks. There, in the distance, was where Trevor had taken his last breath. A headstone. A memorial to many.

We weren't the only ones on the beach, grieving. An older couple clung to each other, both pointing to the rocks. Weeping. Together they approached the slapping waves and tossed a green wreath to the writhing currents. Letting go of what they held dear. Had their loved one also died on the Zephyr?

Zander applied gentle pressure to my shoulders. He'd seen them too. Regardless of the great sins committed that led to Trevor's death, I knew that I needed to release him. I trusted God for Trevor's soul. I took a deep breath and imagined throwing a wreath to float alongside the one already offered. I acquiesced. His time on this earth was done. Zander rubbed my shoulders and linked my arm within his as we turned away from the cold wet grave.

"Shall we? Do you have the map?"

Zander nodded. "I have it memorized. May seem too odd to be poking about with the diagram out in the open." He looked back up to the cliff we'd come down and made a full turn. "The caves are to the left. Matthew said he hid in the one about six entrances down. There." He pointed. "Poor child walked a mile after that treacherous swim."

We hastened as much as we dared and finally came to the cave's mouth. A short, stony trail made for a fairly easy climb. How the wind whipped 'round the rocks! I tightened my bonnet and followed Zander into the darkness.

"This is it, I've no doubt. The cave is located just as he described." He pulled a candle from his coat. "Hold this while I light it."

I followed Zander as he carried the flame around a rock wall. He pushed me back as a scream caught in my throat. Too late.

I'd seen their bodies. The hole dug. The blood everywhere. One a stranger, the other not. Why was she here? *Why?*

He rushed me out of the cave and I clung to a cold jutting rock. I could no longer hold the contents of my stomach. Dear God, what had happened? I sank to my knees and Zander with me. I could not get my breath. Neither could I still my heart nor calm my stomach. "Why, Zander? What had she done?"

He held my forehead as the shocking sight clanged in my mind. Stones dug into my knees and the anger I'd tried so hard to keep at bay again surged.

"We must find the magistrate. Can you stand?" He lifted me to my feet and we walked the mile back to the coast and up to the village. Neither of us voiced aloud what we'd seen. Zander held onto me tightly.

How could it be, how could it be? Aunt Honora was crumpled in that cave. How dare she? How dare she pass from this earth amid a bevy of secrets?

"I should not have brought you. Forgive me, Elaina."

An hour later, we'd given our testimony to the magistrate who'd sent men to gather the bodies. What other arrangements were made, I did not know. Time blurred.

Zander escorted me to our rooms and set a footman at the door. Food sat on a tray, but I could not eat. Nor could I weep.

Voices muffled at the doorway, Zander. He'd returned. The door opened and he approached. "Elaina. I have news. She lives. Your Aunt Honora lives. The doctor is with her now."

I dropped my head to my arms, numb at this new hope. "And that man?"

"He, alas, is dead." Zander placed a hand between my shoulder blades. "Did you know him? Recognize him at all?"

"No."

"I didn't either." He pulled a chair beside me. "We have two options, my love. I can send you home in the carriage now and I will stay and see to things here. This will allow you to get back to Matthew and try to put this unpleasantness behind you. Or, you can stay here, though I loathe to think I've brought you into any sphere of danger. However, depending on Honora's condition, you may wish to be by her side."

I lifted my head. "I am utterly confused."

Zander nodded. "Yes. Pray that she wakens so that we may know the truth." He tapped his fingers on his side. "I've had her placed in one of the lower rooms, and the magistrate has seen that she is guarded. He suspects she may have killed the man."

"Aunt Honora? Kill? Never."

"Perhaps she acted in self-defense."

Why she would need to do such a thing was nothing compared to the fact that she was here, in the very cave we sought. What schemes thrived here? My spirit sank.

Zander pulled something from his pocket. "Elaina. Look."

"The keys?"

He nodded. "They were clutched in Honora's hand."

A new thought. "Carl told Matthew to guard them with his life. Is that what Aunt Honora had done?"

He put them back into his coat pocket. "The sooner she wakes the better."

"I wonder if Carl knows she's here?"

"He may have sent her—or perhaps he is also here. Perhaps he is the one that—"

A knock sounded at the door. Zander opened it. The magistrate. "The woman below rouses. I will be present for any ensuing conversation."

"Yes, of course. We will be down in a moment." Zander closed the door.

"Does the magistrate know our story? Why you are here?"

Zander nodded. "I've been communicating with him these few months."

"Are you ready?"

"As I will ever be." Facing Aunt Honora within nefarious circumstances was proving hard to absorb.

When we entered the room, a sob escaped my throat. She was badly wounded. A nursemaid wiped blood from her chin and the magistrate stood in the corner.

The doctor washed his hands in a bowl of pink-stained water. "No broken bones that I can tell, but she's been socked a good punch to the jaw and eye. The blood on her gown—most of it belonged to the other occupant of that cave. Looks like she hit the back of her head on the cave wall. Maybe some internal bleeding, but I cannot know for certain."

"I see." Zander guided me forward as Aunt Honora's eyes blinked.

"Must be dreaming." Her voice came in a hoarse whisper. "I've died and my dear niece is here beside me?" She teared up. "How I've missed you."

I drew closer to her bed. "You are in Cornwall, Aunt? Wandering about." I brushed matted hair from her bruised eye.

Her hand fastened on mine. "Did you hear too? Did you get a message, dear?"

I looked at Zander, he shook his head and grasped my free hand.

"What is it, Aunt? What brought you to this place?"

"Of course I came with Carl. Where is he? I can't find him. We were together. He—yesterday." She blinked trying to recall. "Yesterday, he claimed we were to bring Matthew home." Her chin quivered. "Someone sent a message that he yet lived. We came to fetch him."

"Oh Aunt..." Zander squeezed my hand in a hard quick pulse. Without a word, I understood. I was not to reveal Matthew's whereabouts.

"But he isn't alive, is he? We've been tricked." Tears coursed down her face. "I knew it was too good to be true, but Carl insisted we come if there were any chance at all."

"Do you know how you ended up in a cave?"

She blinked again, clearly confused. "I—he—where Matthew had been living. That's what the letter said."

Zander stepped close. "Who sent the message?"

"Lord Sherborne." She blinked again. "To think that I was once a beauty of the ballroom. Forgive my disheveled state."

"Who sent the message, Aunt Honora?" I asked.

"Oh. It wasn't signed. But the hand was very elegant indeed." She took a deep breath. "Where is Carl?"

"We haven't seen Carl, but who was the man found with you?"

"What man?"

"Did he accost you?"

I glanced at Zander who looked to the magistrate. The man nodded and stepped out of the room.

"I don't remember. I am so cold. So very cold." The nurse pulled a hot brick from the fire, wrapped it in cloth, and tucked it close to her shivering body. "Dear Elaina, if you didn't get a letter—why ever did you come for me?"

More specifically, how did we find her in the very cave where Matthew had purportedly lived? Though wounded, Aunt Honora's mind was sharp.

Zander stepped in. "We stood on the beach remembering those who were lost. It is uncanny that we found you."

She shuddered again. "I call it providential, my dears." Her eyes blinked heavily as her body warmed from too many hours in the cold. "Providential." Sleep overtook her.

The doctor walked us to the door. "I'll send word if there are any changes."

A guard remained, not that Aunt Honora could go far even if she tried. How she hiked to the cave was beyond my ken. Then again, she did love Matthew and would do anything for him.

We went back to our room where fresh, hot food had been delivered. Much to our relief. We sat and recounted what we knew.

"I want to believe her. I do."

Zander shoveled in a bite of stew. "Her story – what there is of it – makes some sense. But who was trying to draw Carl back here? Whoever it was didn't anticipate an older woman coming along. But why would he bring her? Did he think she'd serve as a shield? He put her in grave danger."

"Not to mention the keys you found her clutching."

"Mm. No doubt Matthew's. Did you notice the dirt beneath her fingernails?"

They had been dirty. I assumed from the struggle.

"The hole in the cave matches Matthew's description." He looked at me with a pointed expression. "I must find Carl."

The bread I chewed became a stone in my stomach. I hoped we would find him before he, too, met his demise.

"Shall I ready the carriage and send you back to Goodwyn?"

I reached across the table and took his hand. "I should prefer to stay with you, my husband."

"On one condition."

"Yes?"

"If I feel it best to send you home at any given time, you will go."

His protective words flowed over me. I would trust them, bask in them. "I agree."

Chapter Nineteen

I slept fitfully. How did anyone bear this rugged, merciless land? The blustering wind never stopped. Zander had made every attempt to keep me warm, including having hot bricks set at my feet and feeding a roaring fire on the hour. For me. He couldn't stop pacing. I wanted nothing more than to be tucked in safely at his side, but it was not to be.

It was obvious that his mind was sifting through everything he knew about Dawes Shipping, the wreck. He noisily shuffled through papers. Grunted. Held his hands before the fire, and finally whispered a prayer. I prayed with him from my bed.

By morning, I blinked awake, not remembering when I'd finally fallen asleep. Zander stood beside the bed, waiting, already dressed.

"I didn't want to leave without telling you."

I reached my hand out. "Thank you."

He held the keys. "I feel I am to hand these over to the magistrate."

"Are you sure?"

"Not entirely. It's been on my mind all night. Prayed about it and couldn't rest until I decided—knew—this is what I'm supposed to do, come what may." His face appeared peaceful. "Sorry if I kept you up."

"Will you go to him right away?" These keys that people might have died for were stained with blood. I wanted no part of them.

"He is downstairs as we speak."

"I will breakfast and spend the morning with Aunt Honora."

He kissed the top of my head. "Good plan. I will see you later—oh, and my love, the footmen will be following you, for your protection should you need it. Do not mind them."

"Thank you, Zander." His attention to my every need touched me.

"If you need me for any reason, send a footman. I'll be in the private parlor."

He left and I once again donned my clothing wondering when this deathly business might be put to rest.

When I entered Aunt Honora's room, she was yelling at the nursemaid. "You've stolen my keys!" Her face was red and spittle flew from her lips. "Where are they?"

I backed away before she could see me.

The guard raised an eyebrow.

"How long has she been like this?"

"For two hours, my lady."

I reentered the room. Her eyes grew wide at my entry. "Dear Aunt. The nurse knows nothing of your belongings. Now, if you give direction to where you were staying, someone may be able to return your things to you." Minus the keys, which were hopefully in the magistrate's hands by now.

"Why...why...why...the tavern. Yes. On the other side of the village." She looked up at me with childlike eyes. "I should like my cap. It is too cold." She shivered.

I opened the door and gave instructions to the waiting footman. He would carry the request to Zander. Maybe someone there would have seen Carl. I wouldn't be surprised if they already thought of such.

I returned my attention to Aunt. "Tell me, how are Lyvia and the children? I daresay she misses your assistance." Lyvia had no other servant other than a cook, which I knew Zander had kindly provided.

She played with a string on the edge of her blanket. "I expected to be home by now with Uncle Matthew to charm them with his stirring tale of survival."

"How is Lyvia?" Why the avoidance?

"Did you know that the Harcourts have been cut?" She smirked. "Serves them right."

No one deserved to be cut unless they were rakes. I blinked at the thought. Being shunned by the Ton had been a blessing in disguise. "Aunt. Tell me of Lyvia."

She sighed. "She is with child and we shall be all the poorer."

"Carl's work supplies, surely." Along with Zander's payments.

"Have I told you how I was the delight of the ballroom when I was young? I captured the eye of every man." Her jaw worked. "How low I have sunk. Shameful, truly so."

I'd often wondered why she'd never married. I had viewed her portrait at eighteen years of age. A beauty to be sure, and seemingly much desired.

"But not a single one captured your eye sufficient for a proposal? Is that the way of it?" Never made sense.

Her eyes flashed. Such a reply used to make her laugh. "He betrayed me."

"The man you wanted to marry?" I cringed at the possible endings to this story.

"On the eve I expected my own engagement announced, it was announced for another."

"How awful."

"Right in the midst of a ball. We'd gathered 'round. I'd been waiting for him to dance with me all evening. Walk me out to the balcony. Propose. I wore peach silk, a string of pearls...I thought he was going to reach for me and pull me to the center of attention. Publicly claim me as his bride..." Her voice trailed off in the memory before snapping back to focus. "He was mine. I was expecting his child."

"Oh Aunt." I took her hand but she pulled it away.

"No one knew." She sniffed. "I went on a year-long European tour along with your own dear parents when they were married. Brought back with us their first child." Tears gathered. "No one suspected." Her chin quivered. "He is gone now. Gone."

Trevor. She meant Trevor.

She clawed at my hands, pulled at my arms. "The letter told me Matthew was alive! My Matthew."

I looked to heaven, beseeching. Didn't know what to think or say. My brother—my dearly loved brother was Aunt Honora's.

"And the father—"

"The *father*," she spat, "is unworthy of the name. The cad continues to bring sorrow. I despise reading about him and his wife constantly in the social column. He ruins those who oppose him, you know. One might refuse a dance and he'd see them cut." Her hand squeezed mine tighter. "I opposed him. And so did your departed mother-in-law."

Lady Sherborne. Banbury? That's who she spoke of. I wouldn't have known if Zander hadn't happened to see him.

A giggle tumbled out. "He will destroy himself, to be sure."

The doctor stepped in with his medical bag and, I hoped, something to calm her. I needed to find Zander.

"Now. Where are my keys, young lady?" Her eyes flashed.

"Aunt? What keys do you speak of? What do they unlock?"

She clutched her blanket and blinked at me slowly. "My inheritance, my dear. *My* inheritance." Whatever did she mean?

The doctor prepared a tincture and indicated by a nod that I should leave. Aunt's inheritance had long ago disappeared. What on earth did she speak of?

I sent the footman for Zander and he joined me in our room. I told him everything.

"Banbury." The name sounded like an expletive on Zander's lips. "How easy he found it to wrong your Aunt long ago, throwing her off with such scant regard."

I folded my arms. "I don't believe he knows that Trevor..."

"I think not. One does not easily condemn a Banbury."

"He is above the law, then."

"More like, akin to the King on the brink of madness."

"Do you think it is a coincidence that Banbury is here?"

Zander walked over to the fire and threw another log on. "I asked the magistrate if he often visits. He apparently keeps regular rooms and—" He looked away. "A mistress."

"Aunt Honora should be glad he didn't propose to her. To think she could be married to such a blackguard." I went to the window. Zander had gone quiet. I knew that it was common for men of the aristocracy to keep a woman, but it was wrong. How painful for their wives. I refused to think of it. Forbade myself.

Zander approached and turned my shoulders to face him. "If I may be frank, my love?"

I nodded. My pulse pounded.

"I have *never,* nor will I ever visit a brothel or maintain a mistress. You are the only one with whom I've ever lain beside on a bed." He smiled. "I promise."

"Thank you for telling me, Zander." Such things a woman knew to never voice. What would happen if she did? He kissed the side of my face.

"Banbury not only besmirched my mother's good name, he sought to ruin mine—though we were hardly acquainted. He spread a rumor that shut every door to any eligible woman in the Ton. The lies spread all the way to Butterton." He shook his head. "Half of the inhabitants were ready to believe anything of me. Took a great while to recover from that."

I pressed a hand to my heart. "Words have such power. I am sorry, Zander."

"Thank God not all of my friends believed."

We took a chair, exhausted from the day. "What did the magistrate say?"

"That he highly suspects the key opened the doors to one of the mines now defunct. Possibly a hiding place for cargo from the shipwrecks. The thieves keep it hidden from the excise men until they can resell without suspicion."

"So Carl..."

"It looks bad for him if he is still alive."

I was angry with Carl. Hurt and confused. But death? Did he deserve that?

"Why would he tell Matthew to guard the keys with his life?"

Zander rejoined. "Why spare anyone's life?"

Carl knew the names of those who had died. Did he read the list and grieve his part in these dark doings?

"Will the magistrate inspect the mines? Find out what has been hidden?" And why Aunt Honora called it her inheritance?

Zander sighed. "He is willing to try, but I sense his unease. These are difficult parts to govern. Once crossed, the sword of Damocles hangs closer to his head. He's called for the militia to come. I agree. Better protection is needed given that a man's been murdered and your Aunt assaulted."

"Did they find out who it is?"

"No one is claiming to know him." Zander unfurled the latest edition of the *London Times*. "Honora must tell the truth. Before anyone else gets hurt."

Chapter Twenty

I tried to gently pry the truth from Aunt Honora. She pretended mindlessness from the medication. The doctor rolled his eyes at her performance. Nothing he'd given her would put her in such a state. She was playing games. But why? As far as new details about Carl, she held to her story of the letter claiming Matthew's existence.

When I asked her about the keys again, "What keys? I have no keys, Elaina."

A knock came to the door and a footman motioned me to the hallway.

"Yes?"

"Lord Sherborne has requested you join him in the lower parlor."

I followed him downstairs. In the center sat two small trunks. Aunt Honora's and Carl's. What did it mean?

The magistrate was there. "You will verify the owners of this trunk and satchel?"

"Of course."

He cleared his throat, "Do sort through your Aunt's things and make a list." He handed me a pencil and some foolscap.

Zander lifted the unlocked lid and I began as they sorted through Carl's. Was distracting, knowing he was nearby and likely hiding. Did he know I was here, too? What if we came face-to-face?

I lifted out a small stack of garments. The rest of the trunk was filled with Matthew's things, along with several rolls of bandages. His favorite books none the worse for wear. Below was the letter, which I handed to the magistrate.

He unfolded the paper and read. "Just as she said. Someone did write of Matthew's survival and whereabouts—I think to lure Carl here."

"If they thought he had the keys—then—"

Zander nodded. "He, quite possibly, wasn't meant to have them."

Confusion abounded. "Aunt Honora—how did she know? Matthew only told us about the keys, with much fear and trembling, if you recall."

Zander blinked slowly. "We aren't the only ones he told, Elaina." He tossed aside Carl's breeches to the floor.

"But..."

"Do Matthew and your Aunt share a close relationship?"

I nodded. "She was like a grandmother to him..." The awful truth dawned. She was his grandmother.

Zander filled in the rest. "Matthew hid for a while before he was found and beaten. Somehow managed to survive. Someone had to help him or he wouldn't have made it. I've been trying to find out who." His mind was whirring. "He must have been so scared. Desperate after losing his father and afraid of his uncle."

I groaned. "He wrote to her. She knew."

The magistrate checked the time on his pocket watch. "Must have told her everything, including details about the keys and where he'd hidden them."

"But then he was beaten and ill…"

"He'd endured too much to remember everything in the right order." Zander sat down in a chair, his long legs stretched out.

"Aunt Honora would have told Carl, thinking she could trust him." Zander's words came back to me *"She opposed the plan…"* The plan of pairing me off with the highest bidder. She knew about it but had not told me.

"No." I bent my head as the shame of my family weighed. "She knew. Just as she knew how Carl was going to make money from bargaining with my life. She knew, yet kept the secrets about Trevor. Why? She is devastated by his death."

The magistrate's lips drew into a large smile. "Has your aunt any difficulty holding liquor, by any chance? Might be what the doctor orders. For her stomach and all…"

Three goblets of wine later, Aunt Honora sang like a shrill lark. I would have laughed if the situation wasn't as grim as it looked. The magistrate and Zander stood on the other side of the door, pencil in hand, waiting for her lips to loosen. On and on she went, singing melodies from her youth, a hiccough between every other line.

Reluctantly, I handed her another half-filled goblet. Any more, and she'd be snoring through tomorrow.

"Mmmmm...." She smacked her lips. "Carly won't let me, won't let me..."

I leaned in.

"Drink wine..." She sang again.

"Where is Carl?"

She shrugged her shoulders. "Lef me. He lef me."

"Did he go with you to the cave?"

"Lef me at the cave. Had to go..."

"Where did he go?"

"Carl hated..." She belched. "Hated what he had to do."

"What did he have to do?"

She sipped the wine again. "Many tings. Too many tings. Poor boy, poor boy. Poor blackmailed boy."

"Blackmailed?" My heart thrummed. How did she know?

Her voice rose in a sing-song sound. "Black-mailed by a black-guard."

"What is your inheritance?"

"Mine." She hiccoughed again. "He owes me."

"Who owes you?"

She leaned way back on her pillows and began to snore.

Zander stepped inside and led me out. "Well done, my love."

"But we still don't know what Carl was doing."

"We know more than we did before.

The night had grown dark and the winds, if possible, more violent than before. We retired to our room, unsettled and on guard. Zander slept in the chair with the pistol by his side.

Hours into the night, a bell clanged a warning, joined by another, and another. Zander lit a lantern and looked from the window. I joined him. "What's happening?"

"Dear God." He looked at me aghast. "A ship has wrecked." He reached for his overcoat and pistol.

"You aren't going out there?"

"I must."

"Zander—no."

"People could be dying. And if no one else in the godforsaken village cares that they survive, I do."

"Do not go alone, I beg you."

"You aren't coming, Elaina. But be ready to help if there are women and children."

He left for the beach and I watched as nearly everyone in the village braved the icy wind carrying lanterns, baskets, and sacks. Some even pushed wheelbarrows. They ran towards destruction like children ran for prizes at a fair.

I prayed for Zander. For the magistrate. For the poor terrified souls who would fly home this night. I bent to my knees and wept. How was it that humanity was so easily lured? *What should I do, Lord?* Shouts arose, loud voices wavered on the wind. The bells continued to ring. No one in the village would sleep tonight.

I dressed, knowing that I'd go see Aunt Honora. I'd watch her sleep if need be, and pray. Fervently. I put my cloak about my shoulders for warmth and carried a candle. I nodded to the footman. "I am going to see my aunt." He followed.

When we arrived at her door, her guard was gone. Had he joined the mayhem? The tavern seemed empty. The footman held a hand for me to wait. He eased open the door and looked to the right and to the left. He nodded. "She is asleep. Best let the sleepin' dog lie, if you ken my meanin'."

"Thank you, Jim." I moved to enter.

"I'll be right here, my lady."

Aunt Honora was in the same position as when I left her, but with her arms stretched wide open. I set my candle on the small table, sat, and observed this once-beauty, snoring in her sleep. For all the noise around her, it was a wonder she didn't wake.

Lord, what would you have me do here?

Wait.

It seemed a woman's lot to constantly wait. I tried not to think of what Zander was doing. Begged God that no harm would come to him. Our love was blossoming...

I waited and waited in the still room while the outside world wrought havoc, man and nature, two wild beasts at play. I woke with a start, I must have dozed off. My candle yet flickered. I heard a noise. A thump and a groan. The door eased open and I held my breath. *Lord.*

A man stood in the shadows. "Jim?"

He shuffled closer, pulling a ragged hood from his head. "Elaina?"

It was Carl.

"You are here to help Aunt Honora." A statement, not a question. He lifted an object. The shine of silver caught the candlelight. A pistol.

Lord. I found my voice. "She's been hurt."

He brought the pistol up, his hand stroked the barrel. "How did you know?"

I took a shaky breath. "I didn't."

"What are you doing here?"

"Sightseeing."

"Did he bring you here?"

"He?"

"Don't be coy, Elaina. It doesn't suit you."

"Did you hurt Jim?"

"Is that his name?" He shook his head. "He won't be out for long."

"What are you doing here, Carl?"

He flicked his chin at Aunt Honora. "What did she tell you?"

I needed to be careful. "That you received a message that Matthew lived. That he was here."

A flash of emotion swept across his face. "They lied. He isn't here." He grit his teeth. "Killed him. They've killed him." He licked his lips. "They sent you the same letter." He took a breath through his nose and wiped his hair from his forehead. "Cruel."

I didn't correct his assumption. "Why did you think you had to sneak inside? Do you not have a right to see Aunt Honora?"

"Where are the keys, Elaina?"

"What keys?"

He moved to Aunt Honora's side and shook her shoulder until she roused. "Get off me, you ruffian!"

"It's me. Carl."

"Carl?" She sat up in bed, blinking. "Would that you died and not Trevor."

"How dare you." His voice was a knife edge.

She stabbed a finger at his chest. "I don't much like you right now. Abandoning me when that awful man attacked."

"I didn't abandon you. I fought and killed him, without a single word of thanks"

I gasped.

She wasn't finished. "And absolutely left me for dead. In a cold, dark cave where I had no business being, mind you."

"I went for help, dear Aunt Honora, and was accosted."

"*Accosted?* You look perfectly fine to me."

I looked closer at him. His wrists were bloodied. His nose appeared to be broken. Held his ribs with one hand. Broken also?

I moved closer to him. "You've been bound? That must have been painful. Carl, let me help you. Bandage your wounds." Anything to keep him here until Zander returned.

"I don't have time for that. I need the keys, Aunt Honora. Now."

She heaved a great sigh. "Gone. I remember having them and then—I didn't."

Carl seemed physically punched by her words. "Dear God." Despair wrenched. "I will hang."

I ventured closer. "Carl? What are the keys for? Why are they important?"

He shook his head.

Aunt Honora wiped her eye. A tear? "My inheritance."

"Of all the twisted—" Carl didn't finish. "He will end me if I don't follow through. If you don't give me the keys, there will be no more Dawes upon this earth. Of this, I've been guaranteed."

Aunt leaned forward, annunciating each word. "I do not have them."

Carl grew quiet, then turned to me. "If Lord Sherborne values your life, tell him to take you home without delay."

Carl? The one who would have thrown my life away for money? He seemed to care. "Before I go, I need to understand. Why were you going to sell me to the highest bidder?" My tone had grown hard.

"How did you—Elaina. I was never going to do that. I was trying to—" His hand drew into a fist. "I was trying to draw someone out."

"And I was the bait?"

"I thought if I could face him—and then..."

Aunt Honora wagged her finger. "Blackmail the blackmailer."

"Was a terrible plan. I should never have used your name. He was not tempted, it seems."

Aunt Honora harrumphed. "Was a good plan, if I say so myself."

"Aunt!" They tangled a web I could hardly traverse.

Carl poured a glass of wine and drank it in one swallow. "Lord Sherborne came out of the blue. I can't tell you how relieved I was. I knew he'd protect you."

"He is a good man, Carl."

"If I were half as good... I am cursed, it seems."

I folded my arms. "Did Aunt Honora say you are being blackmailed?"

"Against such a man, I have no power." He looked from the window, right and left. "I must go."

"What will you do?"

"Tell Lyvia and the children that I love them."

"Carl—no."

His face hardened.

The door opened and Zander stood tall, pistol at the ready. Men stood behind him. "Stand over there, my love."

I moved quickly.

Carl lowered his firearm. "How long have you been listening?"

"Long enough." Zander stepped closer. "Hand me your weapon."

He did.

The scene blurred as tears welled in my eyes.

"Good. Now. How do you fancy being captured by the militia and placed under full guard?"

"I fancy that far more than being a dead pawn."

"Indeed." Zander nodded to the men. "Take him down the hall. I'll be there presently." The men each took Carl by the arm.

"He's being blackmailed."

"So I heard." Zander put his pistol down and drew close. He was wet and no doubt cold.

"How much did you hear?"

"Everything. Well done, Elaina."

"How did you know to come here?"

"You weren't in our room. I knew you wouldn't venture out..."

"What's going to happen?"

"We are going to find out why those keys are so important."

Chapter Twenty-One

"A cache." Carl sat before a full plate of food. "I was to retrieve the goods from the Zephyr's wrecking and carry it to another location."

"Where?"

"I don't know. A man is—was supposed to meet me there with a wagon."

"How did you know it would happen tonight?"

"I was informed."

The magistrate looked to his secretary who recorded the details as fast as he could. "Get that?" The man slapped his mug of ale on the table. "You had knowledge that lives would be lost and did not inform anyone."

Zander pulled papers from his satchel. "And these manifests? And routes?"

"The game is so much bigger than you know. Stick around much longer, and he will draw you in whether you want to be or not."

"How was he blackmailing you?"

"At first, he threatened my wife if I did not concede."

"How did he do that?"

"And he would call my debts if I didn't succeed." Carl picked at the bread. "Which he did do. Regardless of the Zephyr's...success."

"How did you get away from the men that held you captive."

"I got away."

"Set you free, did they?" The magistrate narrowed his eyes.

Zander waved paper in the air. "Why did you have manifests from other ships?"

"Dawes Shipping wasn't the only one being blackmailed."

The magistrate paced. "You are telling me that this unknown man has made a game of forcing shipping companies to wreck their own ships?"

"Yes. We are required to race. The ship that comes in last agrees to be wrecked..."

"You make me ill."

"He was going to kill me if I didn't participate."

The magistrate slammed the table. "Thirty souls to your guilt, Mr. Dawes. You were willing enough that they should die."

Carl sniffed. "I hoped they would be saved."

"A paltry hope."

"We had to race for the keys in London—then race to the cache."

No wonder Carl had told Matthew to guard them with his life. No wonder he'd been tortured and left for dead.

"Who were you racing against here?"

"Locals."

"I see."

Zander stepped away from my side. "Why did you not confide in Trevor?"

Carl looked away.

He'd always been a gentleman, if somewhat aloof at times. Now, he sat covered in filth and blood. Pain etching his face.

The magistrate nodded. He knew something. "What was in it for you, if you fulfilled your task?"

"The life I lived before."

"Wealth?"

Carl nodded. "Enough..."

Aunt Honora's inheritance. I cringed. Her complaints over the years—our fall from society had been difficult for her. The entire family had been embarrassed, but she, the longest accustomed to fine things, had to do without. We thought her a silly, old woman. How little we understood.

Carl, too, had suffered disgrace, bitter over our losses. Never accepted the truth—or the goodness of our situation. While often hard, I felt that I'd truly begun to live.

The magistrate pointed to his secretary's notes. "So, as I have recorded here, your life hung between the unequal balance of a threat to your wife and your life—and that of great wealth. Why protect the man behind these machinations?"

Carl shouted. "Because I have a wife and children!"

Carl did know. He intimated as much in Aunt Honora's room. He knew exactly whom he tried to draw out.

Zander stepped from the room, pulling me with him. He spoke to the men waiting. "Hasten to London, inform the guards there. Increase the watch."

"Zander. You posted a guard for Lyvia?"

"I was afraid for her and the children."

I squeezed his hand. "It is Banbury, isn't it?"

"I don't know, but I intend to find out."

I grew sick to my stomach.

"The guards will do their job. Lyvia will be safe."

Zander waved the magistrate to join us in the hall. "Lord Banbury. You said he comes here often."

The magistrate wiped his eyes with his handkerchief. "Too often for my liking."

"We should go to him. Now."

"The streets are overrun. I will pay a visit to his quarters first thing in the morning." He looked back at my brother, the captive. "There is more I need to know."

Zander nodded in agreement. "Morning is but a few hours away. I will be ready." He placed my hand on his arm but turned back to the magistrate. "Before we arrived, we dined at Butterton Hall. Lord Camden invited me to place a bet. On shipping companies. Called it a horse race."

"A horse race? You've got to be kidding me. Is the whole of the gentry involved?"

"I dearly hope not."

"Haven't seen Camden in several years. But he never could turn down a wager. Such weakness." He turned to me. "My lady, you've been a great help to us. You have my gratitude."

It felt very strange to be thanked for continuing the Dawes's downfall. Zander led me upstairs and bade me to sleep. I crawled beneath the blankets, fully clothed, while he donned fresh garments.

My eyes were raw and heavy. "It is both better than I realized—and much, much worse."

Zander stood beside the bed and stroked my unbound hair. "How so?"

"Did you hear? He wasn't going to sell me. He was attempting to draw out his blackmailer." Why had it made sense a few hours ago, but not now?

"How does one go about blackmailing a blackmailer?"

"By knowing something he doesn't realize you know—or having something that can incriminate him for financial extortion."

"How would using my name—"

"Banbury doesn't tend to resist women he is presented with."

"He must have missed the memo that went around the clubs."

"By the grace of God."

"Zander, Carl seems to fear him. How did he think facing him would benefit?"

He ran his fingers down the length of my hair. "Do not think about it."

But I couldn't stop. "If I became his mistress—then I would be able to find out things."

"And Carl might have had a fighting chance at stopping him."

"He lied to me."

"He didn't want you to think the worst of him." Zander paused mid-stroke. "Banbury's mistress...you've caught on to something important. The magistrate can help. We must speak with her."

"Is there someone looking out for Aunt Honora?" How Carl's plan must have disgusted her! But then, hadn't she said that it was her idea—and a good one at that?

"I left a footman in charge of the door. Poor Jim—he's got a large goose egg and a terrible pain."

I pushed the covers back and got out of bed. "I think it wise to check on her."

"After the night we've had, you're right."

When we got to her room, the footman was bound and gagged, and Aunt Honora nowhere to be seen.

Zander freed him.

"Blasted old woman!" The footman wiped his mouth. "I'm sorry my lord. I fell asleep and she bound me. Then aimed that pistol at me. Nothing I could do."

"A pistol?" Zander closed his eyes. "How did she manage it?"

"Oh Zander." He was exhausted from the beach rescue. He hadn't been thinking about the cost he'd pay for such bravery.

"If Banbury is responsible for Trevor's death—do you think she's gone to see him?"

"God help us if she has." He grabbed my hand. "We've no time to lose."

We hurried to the magistrate who grimaced at the news. "So much misfortune in one night!"

The streets had died down and the bells had grown quiet. Zander held my hand tightly and whispered in my ear. "You may be able to handle your aunt better than either of us. But if she isn't peaceful, and is waving the pistol about—you must run back to our rooms."

I nodded. Aunt would be outraged.

The Exeter had been abandoned as much as our inn had been. Servants milled aimlessly. Aunt Honora might have climbed the stairs without notice.

The magistrate led the way, up the two long flights and down the hall. We tucked ourselves against the wall as he softly knocked. No answer. A louder knock. "Banbury? Sorry to wake you at this ungodly hour." Still nothing.

He turned the handle. "Unlocked." He pushed the door open. "What's this?"

We entered behind him. Aunt Honora sat with Zander's pistol cradled against her chest.

"He's gone." Her chin quivered. "I wanted to kill him for what he has done to me and my family." She held out the gun. "Isn't loaded, you see?"

Zander swiped it from her grasp.

"I pointed it straight at him, but he knew I didn't know how these things work. He laughed and knocked it from my hands as though such violence was merely a whim. Everything is a whim to him. Everything."

I wrapped my arms around her shivering form.

"He killed Trevor and Matthew. Countless others. He must pay. And if the Crown will not execute such a coward – a criminal..." She pointed her finger at the magistrate, "Then you must." She turned to Zander. "Or you."

She leaned her head against my shoulder, weeping. "His manservant held a dagger to my throat while they gathered up his belongings."

The magistrate's eye twitched. "How long ago?"

"An hour? I scarcely know."

Zander stepped to the end of the room to an east-facing window. A large brass telescope sat upon a desk. He lifted some paper. "He's made notations. Can't make them out."

"Ms. Dawes—where was Banbury when you entered the room?"

"At the spyglass."

"Indeed."

Zander peered through the lens. "I'll wager that what I see here is the mine where the cache is hidden."

The magistrate took a turn. "Wyndam—it's been abandoned for ten years. The landlord is aged. Doesn't go near the place anymore. When the militia arrives, we will take the keys and try the door."

Aunt Honora thrust herself out of my hold and stood. Fury unfurled across her brow. "You have my keys?"

"What know you, woman, about keys?"

Her back straightened and her chin rose. "Whatever is in that mine belongs to the Dawes family."

"Does it now? And those who entrusted Dawes Shipping to carry the product to port? Do they not have a say?"

"My inheritance. Mine." Aunt Honora's tragedy had addled her brain. "I sank every bit of my last farthings into Dawes Shipping. Everything I had. And he knew it. Somehow, he knew! Paid me a visit."

"When?"

Aunt Honora looked at me, then Zander. "Was after you left to carry luncheon to Trevor and Carl—those months ago. I'd sent him a letter, you see. He *owed* me. For decades of heartbreak. He made me a, what shall we call it? A loan. I had information that would see him embarrassed."

"Trevor." His name spilled from my lips.

"Yes. Trevor. And Matthew, his grandson. He has no sons, you see. No heirs." She trembled, unsteady. "There are many among our acquaintances that knew of the...affections we once shared."

Zander folded his arms. "Did he know about Trevor?"

"I never told him. He was only aware that he had a son, of whose whereabouts I alone knew."

I swallowed. "Does Carl know this?"

"Why should I tell him? Would that Carl had died instead. A filthy muck he's made of everything."

One thing became clear. "You tried to blackmail him before Carl's attempt—and failed."

She put a hand to her head. "Yes. He played along as though he were afraid I could upend him. But he wasn't afraid... Not really."

He'd upended the entire Dawes family instead.

"He owes me *everything*. Wealth for wealth...." She choked on her words. "Life...for life." She swayed, then crumpled to the floor.

We lifted her to the bed. I patted her cheeks. "Aunt Honora. Wake up. Come now."

Minutes later, smelling salts were waved beneath her nose. Zander pressed her wrists and put two fingers to her throat. Blood trickled from her mouth, down her chin.

"Aunt Honora! Wake up!"

I needed her to wake. I needed to tell her that life could be good and dear without wealth and rank. Indeed, it had been dear. She needed to know that she might not have had Banbury's love or society's honor, but she had mine. She had my forgiveness. She had thanks for everything she'd done for me as I'd grieved my parents' passing.

She needed to know that Matthew lived. That if she would but look to the Son, by whose stripes she might be healed... Tears welled, unbidden. I couldn't stop them. "Aunt Honora. Reach for God. Cling to Him. Don't ever let go."

I don't know how long I leaned over her. Waiting, hoping.

Zander wrapped his arms around me, pulling me close. "She has left. Let her go, my love."

I turned into his chest and wept.

Chapter Twenty-Two

I was in a daze—or rather, thought I ought to be. I wanted to be blissfully unaware of the many griefs that chased me like ravenous wolves. Instead, I was very much aware—too aware—of everything that had happened and what was yet to occur.

Though we tried, we could not sleep the few hours after dawn.

The militia arrived. The presence of the red-jacketed troops calmed the town's bustle and noise. People didn't stop to talk as they passed each other, and very little business seemed to take place. Villagers stayed out of sight and for good reason. Hiding stolen goods and ill-gotten gains? Shame must hide its face or else the truth might be seen. Was as though a pox had overtaken the townsfolk.

I felt safer. And Zander was relieved. We both stood at our room's large window of frost-edged panes. It had grown even colder. We watched as Carl was taken, hands bound behind his back, and marched to their encampment. He'd agreed to cooperate, regardless of his own survival. What exactly were his crimes? Who knew? According to the law, the details were murky at best. He'd killed a man in self-defense, he claimed. His ship's captain had driven the Zephyr to the rocks. The game he played, he played alone. Live or die, it was out of his control. Carl expected to hang. I couldn't think about that now.

Zander said nothing and I was grateful. He pulled me to his chest again and prayed for Carl—and for Lyvia and the children. One hand cradled my head, the other rubbed my aching back.

We'd bury Aunt Honora at the local kirk tomorrow. My head pounded at the thought. Tears threatened.

A knock at the door. Servants hauled in a large copper tub and several buckets of hot water.

"I've ordered a bath for you, and after that a good meal. Mrs. Pierce is here to help you get settled." Such thoughtfulness.

"Mrs. Pierce?"

"The innkeeper's wife. She's a good sort."

I had to admit, despite the swirling circumstances, a long soak sounded incredible. Something I needed.

"And you are going with the magistrate and the militia?" To open the mine.

"I am."

"What about Banbury's mistress?"

"Nowhere to be found."

"Of course she isn't." If she had a shred of intelligence, she would leave that dangerous man far behind. Perhaps she fled for fear of her life.

"Enjoy your bath." Zander kissed my forehead. "I'll be back in a few hours."

The servants had filled the tub and Mrs. Pierce, a rosy-cheeked woman who seemed to wear happiness in every expression, carried in a vial of rosewater and poured it out liberally. She left me with a cake of soap, a stack of towels, and a freshly laundered gown. "Ring if you need me, dear."

The water's sweet scent and warmth enveloped me. I plunged my head beneath. Comfort, rest, and mercy. Why didn't Aunt Honora partake of these good gifts? Or Carl? I came up as hot tears blended with the water. Comfort, rest, and mercy washed them away.

I dried my hair by the fire thinking and praying for Lyvia, my nieces, and my nephews. What would become of them if Carl was convicted and imprisoned? Or hung as expected? They would be fatherless. Lyvia, even in her patient forbearance would be tested. Devastated. She loved him. If only I could keep the pain far from her. But that didn't seem likely.

I knew Zander would do what he could for her. Was his nature.

I dried my hair by the fire, stroke by stroke, attempting patience as I waited for Zander. The hot food arrived and I ate my fill. I hadn't thought I could eat a bite after what happened. Emotions of every sort came flowing out of me. The grief, yes, in torrents. And love. My love for my family. My increasing love for Zander, my bastion of strength. What great purposes he aspired to accomplish. *Mercy on us, Lord. Grant us mercy.*

Zander flung the door open. "Elaina." He offered a small smile. "Enjoy your bath?"

"It was a gift."

"I'm glad."

"What of the mine?"

"The keys unlocked every door. And revealed the enormous cache."

"And? The conclusion?"

Zander pulled papers from his satchel. "The shipping manifest from the Zephyr's last load—doesn't match what's there."

"Oh my."

"The list states spirits and tea. The crates, my dear, hold French-made weapons."

"Where was Carl supposed to take them?"

"He didn't know. He expected the goods to be his to keep—thought getting them meant he had won that round and Banbury would finally leave him alone."

"If Carl had the keys and opened the doors then..."

"He wouldn't be alive."

"But what did Carl expect to do with such weaponry?"

"I loathe to answer that question. But no two ways about it, the sale would have made him inordinately wealthy. Except, of course, he would have been double-crossed. His part in the game expired. I'm sure of it."

My comb caught a knot and I winced. "Either way, they would have killed him."

"They needed the keys—he had them."

I set the comb down to plait my hair. "Doesn't make sense."

"Remember—this wasn't merely about thievery and smuggling. It's been a twisted game from the start, filled with manipulation, betting...God knows what else."

"Matthew said that Trevor and Carl fought back. Do you think he figured out what was in the crates?"

"He must have seen something—maybe pried open a crate. Knew for a fact that they weren't carrying what they were supposed to be. We'll never know."

"If only Aunt Honora hadn't thought she could best Banbury and gain personally by it..." I squeezed my eyes shut. "Maybe he wouldn't have targeted Carl."

Zander set a hand on my shoulder. "As soon as your aunt is buried, we will travel to London. See to your sister-in-law—and—I must begin listening to the men of the Ton. What kind of wagers they've been placing. I'd like to know how far Banbury's reach goes."

He stroked my cheek with the back of his knuckles. "I can't wait to go home. We've had a rough few days. I want to be alone with you." He took each of my hands and kissed the rings. "I've sent one of the footmen ahead of us to London to prepare the townhouse."

"You have a townhouse in London?" He never stopped surprising me.

"Yes, we do," Zander said. "*We* also have a small estate in Scotland. What's mine is yours, Elaina."

Zander and I spent the rest of the day commiserating with the magistrate, officers, and the excise man. I told all I knew of Dawes Shipping, my brothers. Carl—Aunt Honora. My simple tale added little to the bleak discussions.

Zander gave his own accounts of his dealings and losses—even what his family had endured at the hands of Banbury.

He gave an encouraging nod when they asked yet again about Matthew, why he had the keys. Had I seen them before in London? No—on all counts no.

I saw the open crates of weapons—the silver casts and iron triggers, blade, bayonet, and pistol. Made to both defend and kill. They'd done their damage. More than thirty lost souls, Trevor, Aunt Honora... What a tragic list.

How many had died from the wrecking last night? I hadn't dared to ask.

The next day, Aunt Honora was buried. Only Zander and I attended. With the kind vicar's words, a prayer, and two handfuls of dirt upon the coffin lid, we said our final goodbye.

Moments later, we were blanketed together within the coach to London.

Chapter Twenty-Three

Our visit with Lyvia shocked me. She had been waiting for Carl—he was late. Why had we come? Where was her husband? The children clung to me. They seemed to sense that something was amiss. We stayed until they were tucked into bed and the fear in Lyvia's eyes abated. My poor sister-in-law had been as ignorant as I.

We did not tell her that Matthew lived. Zander thought it best to wait. Just in case. Not that he had anything to fear from Lyvia. Banbury had threatened her, and might still attempt more harm, though she did not say. Time *might* tell if she spoke the truth. Or had something to hide.

After Aunt Honora's and Carl's actions, I wasn't sure who I could trust.

While Zander spoke with the guards, I begged Lyvia to let me stay and help with the children. She wouldn't allow it. She'd grown tight-lipped and quiet. Had little to say though I'd loved her and the children since they'd become a part of the Dawes family. Perhaps she resented her years with Carl. What could I do for her? I had to leave her alone until she wanted my help.

We settled into Zander's—our—townhouse, a fine establishment that was impeccably run by a small staff. Lady Sherborne, it seemed, had it redone but five years prior and abandoned it when she'd rejected Banbury's advances and endured the spread of his malicious gossip. How despondent she must have been.

Over the course of a few weeks, Zander went out every day for long hours—visiting old acquaintances, dropping in on clubs. Each day he returned weary. Hardly anyone would talk—or admit—to Banbury's schemes. But little by little, gentlemen paid visits. Left cards. Begged my husband's company. Name by name, his list grew. As did trust.

A stack of affidavits were drawn up—statements from gentlemen high and low. Owners of businesses—and the other shipping companies did the same. Dealings and bets crossed and tangled, but led undeniably to one man – and one man only. The undercurrent of truth was about to rise to the surface, and Banbury would go down. Zander was sure of it.

He looked up from the morning paper as the mail had been carried in. "An invitation..." He scowled. "To a ball." He handed it to me. "I am loathe to accept."

I read the names of the host and hostess. "The Swanfords?"

"Seems I've caught Swanford's attention. He's an old friend of Banbury's—and had more than a little to share about Banbury's exploits—all conveniently through his solicitor."

"Is it wise to go? You've been so careful. The fear Banbury has instilled in people is palpable." I turned the invitation over. A message scrawled across the back. "Oh look, it seems we've been particularly requested."

I handed it back to Zander. *"It would do us great honor to make the acquaintance of your bride. We look forward to your presence, you cannot miss."*

"Interesting. We should attend."

My mind swam. To be among the Ton again…the vicious, cutting ton. "As long as I am with you." I swallowed. "You aren't afraid to be in the public?"

"No—the evidence I've built is significant and in the right hands. If anything, he will stall some of the activities he's planned. Bets on ships have already stopped." Zander patted my hand. "There isn't a target on my back."

But *I* was afraid. The man had destroyed my family—they had been too afraid to defy him. They leaned into their fear and let it control their choices. Carl sat in a prison in Cornwall, wounded, freezing, and awaiting final judgment.

"How can you be sure?" I knew that Zander hadn't only posted guards for Lyvia's safety, but around our home too.

"He will not touch me."

That did not satisfy.

"Your expression—you do not believe what I tell you?"

"I've lost too much. My sister by way of elopement. My parents. Trevor—almost Matthew. Aunt Honora. Maybe Carl. Lyvia, who won't speak to me no matter how I try. And those dear children by way of their mother's angst."

Zander folded his arms. "Your sister lives—and very happily I might add."

"How do you—" What did he know?

"Matthew must live with us, of course. I look forward to seeing the man he becomes." His gaze caressed my face. "I have hope for Carl. His and your aunt's choices have brought about far-reaching ramifications, but all is not lost. Elaina, your parents and Trevor are with God. You may be secure in that."

"And Lyvia needs time."

"She may not desire to see you right now, but she may be encouraged in other ways. Send her notes. Tell of your love and prayers for her and the children. Leave her in no doubt of your steadfast devotion. When she is ready, she'll know whom to trust."

What had he said about my sister? "Zander. How do you know of my sister's whereabouts?"

"She and her husband are in my employ." His smile widened and his eyes glinted. "I did mention that we have an estate in Scotland?"

How did this come about? "She is happy? Safe?" My heart could not stand this. How I missed her!

He winked. "Not every elopement is a terrible idea..."

At that moment I realized that we'd cut her off as the Ton cut us. *I* cut her off. She left me to pick up the many pieces left behind by her choices and I...She...

The ridiculous pieces and things I'd once thought important, but no longer. Our downfall wasn't entirely her doing. The gossip and the taint of it, for certain. But Father's financial problems were the crux of the issue. Completely. I wondered at my own thoughts. Apparently, her marriage wasn't a taint, but I had thought it to be. Where was my faith?

"I must make amends." My voice had grown hoarse. My family wasn't as far gone as I'd supposed. "How could I disown my sister?" I shook my head. "She hasn't written to us, you know."

"Not true. She wrote to Trevor."

"Is this how she came to work for you?"

He nodded. "She is reluctant to force herself upon you. She feels responsible for your inability to make a good match." His lips quirked a smile.

"Such a devastating turn that's taken. I'm hopeful that one day everything might work out."

He pulled me to my feet and tugged me close. Many days since he'd given me any real notice…or a tender touch. "Utterly and completely devastating." His eyes dropped down to my lips and back up again. "I don't think I'll ever recover."

My voice dropped to a whisper. "Your manservant is outside the door."

"Mm." He kissed me anyway. "Let it be known that Lord Sherborne truly and deeply loves his wife."

Indeed. I felt his love in every word, every deed. Did he feel mine?

He turned to his manservant who delivered a message. "Look, Elaina. We've received another invitation, this one to dine with the cream of the Ton, Lord Banbury himself. Well, now. I have gained his full attention."

My hands rose to my throat.

"Don't be distressed. We won't accept. However, I am glad to have another sample of his unique handwriting to add to my collection."

"When will he be confronted?" The sooner the better.

"As soon as I gain an audience with the King—"

"But he isn't well! Mentally unstable at best!"

"And if not by way of King George, the chief of the constabulary is itching to see the task through. However, the confrontation would be best given King George's permission to touch one such as he."

"Would that his son might rule instead."

"Indeed."

Time grew tight with expectation. The stroke of the clock nearly drove me mad for waiting. A fine thing, then, to have to prepare for a ball. A long hour bathing, two long hours dressing my hair. Another, slipping into a blue silk gown procured with haste from the drapers.

My maid had worked wonders. When I met Zander on the stairs, his eyes took in my length as I took in his. Never had a more handsome man existed.

Did we still court? No—we were engaged. Most certainly. His sweet game of taking time for our relationship to grow blurred with a new passion and hope. His words tantalized.

"Honeymoon? In Scotland?" A kiss to my jaw. A strand of garnets around my neck. A kiss to the clasp. The servants in the foyer were suitably scandalized.

My heart beat in quick succession as he handed me into the carriage. I knew that as soon as the door closed, his lips would be on mine. My husband...

My beloved.

Chapter Twenty-Four

We stood in a lengthy reception line within a large, marble foyer. The door opened and closed with the arrival of guests, the clopping of horse hooves on brick streets, carried inside, mixing with the low gurgle of voices. A mint's worth of candles glowed. Footmen stood in powdered wigs, ready to serve.

Of this portion of the Ton, I had never associated. Such heights were too far above me—up the strand, elegance and beauty became less than parentage, but rather a prize procured at great cost. I recognized some who had moved on the outer edges of this sphere—and some who moved within it. This was no masquerade, yet it was. Wholly and completely.

We approached the Swanfords with the obligatory bow and curtsy. Mr. Swanford bowed over my hand. "Lady Sherborne, Lord Sherborne, you have both been too long from society." He winked.

I looked to Zander and turned my attention back to Lady Swanford. How did he know that I had not been circulating within the lower spheres? Zander placed my hand back within his arm and tightened his hold.

We moved into the ballroom, the path opened before us as murmurs sounded behind fans—and a few men sent my husband acknowledging nods. None came to speak. We walked a slow circle around the opulent room until Zander seated me and stood behind my chair.

"Shall we further scandalize society and dance three dances in a row?"

"They would have us married by the end of the third, my lord."

He laughed a low rumble and I rather panicked. I hadn't danced in a very long time. I was out of practice. The music began and he pulled me to my feet. We joined the line and went through the motions, memory coming back to my hands and feet, grasp to grasp, turn and cross, promenade. Such fun! Each touch meaning more than the next. Each meeting of eyes and I knew that I could never love anyone but him.

The end of the dance came too soon and he led me off the floor, his low voice meant for my ears only. "Would that we had danced your first season, I might not have ever recovered."

Soon after, Zander introduced me to old acquaintances who did their best to figure out who I was and where he'd found me.

"Your maiden name, my lady?"

"Dawes, sir."

"Dawes?"

"Indeed."

"Lady Sherborne, do let me introduce you to my niece, Miss Davies."

And so on, and so on. One old gentleman asked me to dance, to which Zander replied that my card was filled and pulled me onto the floor himself for a waltz, a dance I'd performed but once. Floating around the floor with his arms about me—a few years ago, I would have swooned after the first steps. How different it is to dance with one's love rather than someone who is measuring the potential for compatibility or mere merriment.

The music died down and movement shifted at the door. Late arrivals. Zander pulled me behind a column. "It's Banbury and his wife. Don't worry—in this crush, we can easily avoid speaking with him."

Nerves wrapped around my stomach. I would beg to leave. "Zander—"

"Do you know, most of the gentleman here has offered testimony against him..." His brow furrowed. "Nearly everyone has." His mouth pressed in a line.

Banbury's constant games...were we in the middle of one now?

I gained a good look at him for the first time. His face carried a practiced smile, his bearing as large and powerful as it must have been in his youth. His wife's hand perched on his arm, the feathers in her hair not reaching his height. Much of the crowd bowed as they passed. Others did not. A significant slight.

Zander pulled me farther behind the columns and down from the center. Music began again and Banbury was first to the line set within the middle—a different, much younger woman in tow. His wife seemed not to notice.

I glanced at Lady Banbury, whose feather mane had joined others along the edges of the room.

"Might we take our leave?"

"It is too soon, we may give offense to our hosts."

"I might be developing a headache."

A hand tapped my shoulder. The gentleman from earlier. "Are you, indeed, the former Miss Elaina Dawes?"

His companion's eyebrows rose as the inquiry brooked no answer but one.

"Sir." I curtsied.

"I say, a run of bad luck in your family." Bluntly put.

Or perhaps, a series of bad choices coupled with Banbury's schemes. Zander took my hand. "And a run of good blessing, thank God."

He eyed Zander. "I should say." He walked away, laughing under his breath. Ah, Lord Sherborne had been taken in by a pretty face with ill connection. He should have known better than to marry me.

"Shall I challenge him to a duel or argue that I am the one who is blessed by this arrangement of ours? I should have said so." Regret filled his eyes. "And I think you are right. We don't belong in this place. Not anymore."

Something strange was happening. Shouts blared from the foyer. A man in work attire stumbled into the ballroom, his eyes roved about. He ran towards the middle, his face red. Footmen ran after him, a hand grasped him by the elbow, but he shook it off.

The man pulled a pistol from beneath his coat, waved it in the air. The dancers disbanded and women screamed. Zander shoved me behind him as we tried to get farther away. The man stopped in front of Banbury then cocked and aimed, unsteady on his feet. Drunk.

Banbury rolled his eyes and knocked the weapon to the ground as though a toy. It fired, blasting a floor-length mirror into a thousand shards. My own scream lodged within my throat as Zander put me farther away from the action.

"Stay behind me," Zander commanded. I clung to the fabric of his coat and peered behind his shoulder.

More people fled as the man stumbled and knelt at Banbury's feet and shouted. "I'm sorry. I'm sorry. I can't...I can't do it anymore. Please don't make me. I'll die first!"

Banbury tossed back a full glass of wine and smiled as though distressed men groveled before him every day. Then his expression melted, his face paled. The glass slipped from his hands and shattered on the floor. He grasped his throat and in a few quick choking breaths, crumpled to the floor.

Dear God—what had just happened?

More people ran from the room through the many open doorways. Some men circled Banbury, but did not help. In unison, they chanted, "Judgement, judgement, judgement, judgement..." Oh so briefly. But I'd heard it—like the completed chime of the clock. They parted and stepped away from the man who lay as still as death.

The one who had threatened with the gun was now trapped by the footmen. He did not struggle but shouted, "I didn't kill him! I didn't do it!"

I looked at Lady Banbury, who sat still as a lonely statue. Where were her friends? She looked about for anyone—those who were left to witness the scene had either turned their backs to her or vacated the room. Scandal. Intrigue. Cut.

Did she not care a whit for her husband? Why did she not rush to him? I could only guess at the life she'd had to endure. The prison Aunt Honora had avoided and somehow resented for the rest of her life.

"Stay close, Elaina." Zander ran to him and knelt to take his pulse. "Send for a doctor!" He looked at me and gave a slight shake of his head. It was over. Banbury was dead.

Still, Lady Banbury didn't move, her eyes affixed on the bent form of her husband. Her jaw worked and she gripped her fan. I moved from the column, making my way to the empty row of chairs, and sat beside her.

I'd never made her acquaintance, but I could not leave. To have been married to such a man must have been...I couldn't imagine. It didn't make sense, though, why she was alone. Moments ago, women sought her favor. Now she was a pariah.

I spoke the words I'd given Aunt Honora, were it not too late. "Hold fast to God, Lady Banbury."

Her intake of breath shuddered and she looked at me. "Who are you?"

"Someone who cares." This woman would fall far in the wake of her husband's transgressions. Would she bear it well? How would her life be shaken by his death and subsequent revelation of his crimes? How much did she know?

"I think he is deceased." Her cultured voice gave no indication of regard for the man. No tinge of regret.

A doctor now knelt by the man's side and then quickly covered his face with a handkerchief. Lord Banbury was truly gone.

Lady Swanson and her maids came for Lady Banbury and took her from the scene. Zander stood talking with other gentlemen, all expressing disbelief.

No murder occurred. Banbury drank his wine and collapsed. I had hoped for his power over people to end. I had envisioned him being handcuffed and marched to prison. I had desired retribution. Even execution.

Would that he had repented before the last swallow.

Before it was too late.

Chapter Twenty-Five

The ballroom emptied before Zander was ready to leave. It wasn't until we were in the carriage that he voiced aloud what had most piqued my curiosity. "We'd been particularly invited—and at the last minute too. Almost as if Swanford wanted us to witness Banbury's death."

"How could one plan such an outcome?"

"Easily."

"What about the strange man with the pistol?"

"One of Banbury's pawns. A man who felt cheated. Said he'd been paid handsomely to kill him. Couldn't do it."

"And whoever hired him thought he might fail, so poisoned his wine?"

"A grim possibility—hard to prove."

"Some of the gentlemen chanted. Did you hear them, Zander?"

He nodded and looked out of the dark window. "They had much to lose if our case wasn't strong enough to convict him."

"But it was enough!"

Zander rubbed his eyes. Months of stress and work, weeks of working hard to gain on Banbury. "Yes. I believe so. Only I suppose he crossed the line too far and..." he shook his head. "Justice caught him by the throat."

"We will never hear his confession."

"I don't think he ever would have told the truth. We were banking on testimonies against him."

"What about Carl—what will happen to him?" I had to daily pray for and forgive him. Trying to love him for the brother he'd once been and perhaps could be again...

"He will be held until trial—could be several months away." He cradled my hand in his. "I cannot guess the extent of Carl's activities beyond what he's confessed in our hearing. I hope, with all sincerity, that he is not guilty of more."

Time would tell how many guilty men were left bobbing in Banbury's wake.

"My solicitor has charge of the files and affidavits. Banbury is dead." He shook his head, still in disbelief. "I think we may return home very soon, Elaina." His eyes brightened.

"Can it be as simple as that?"

"Nothing about our lives together has been simple so far, has it? Always a question hounding us. Sorting out seemingly senseless situations. I had no idea it would lead to Banbury—or what Carl thought he had to do to regain his wealth."

"What came first, Zander? Did Banbury first manipulate Carl or was it only when Carl couldn't repay his debt to him that he had an opening? Or was it when Aunt Honora sought to blackmail him and it backfired, badly?"

"Carl couldn't repay him—but neither could several small companies such as Dawes Shipping. Trevor didn't know of the debt because it was personal, separate from the company. What was supposed to be used for the company, he lavished on his family."

For Lyvia and the children. They had no idea.

"And Aunt Honora unwittingly involved herself in a game far more dangerous than she knew."

"Sadly, very true."

"Did Carl think himself so powerful?"

"His confidence rested solely on his wealth. His power grew because others were willing to be a slave to him. Greed will double-cross every man. Even the one who thinks he wields it as a master will find himself a slave instead. Hasn't it always been so?"

"Do you really think Lord Swanford poisoned him? Or paid someone to do so?"

Zander took a deep breath. "I'm not sure I want to know. There will be an inquiry—some candid observations made. I've done all I can."

"Our work is truly finished, then?" I dared not believe this could be true.

"Until Carl goes to court—I may be required to testify."

Still so many questions were unanswered. Mayhap this was the end to our part in righting wrongs. Thoughts ran through my mind. Hopes too. "May we finally tell Lyvia about Matthew?"

"News of Banbury's death will take time to get around. I need to be certain his assailants aren't still trying to find him."

"But the keys were already found and—"

"Don't you think it strange that the men who took Carl left him with naught but raw wrists and a broken nose? But the ones who took Matthew tortured him nearly to death."

I'd thought they were one and the same. Why hadn't they treated the two men alike?

Zander continued. "There's something else at play here. Something more valuable. Something worth killing for..."

"Do you think Matthew told us the complete truth?"

Zander tapped his chin. "I think Matthew may have withheld information. I don't blame him, he's endured a great deal and has many reasons to fear."

Carl seemed only interested in the keys. "Do you think Carl can tell us what he may be hiding?"

"I think that whatever Matthew has concealed may need to stay hidden. For his sake as well as ours. Revealing what he knows may only lead his assailants to his door."

"What if it helps Carl?"

"He may seem eager to tell the truth now— now that justice is served regardless of his punishment. He has no reason left to withhold any information. No—I think that Matthew may have stumbled upon something he wasn't supposed to see, after the wrecking. He doesn't hide more keys or treasure, or anything of the like. He holds knowledge he is loathe to remember. He fears the power he holds."

"And if it may save another's innocent life?"

He gently squeezed my hand. "In that case, we carefully urge him toward honesty upon our return to Goodwyn."

The carriage stopped.

"We are going home?" I felt drawn back to where our lives had barely begun to take root. There was something about the old abbey, the land that surrounded it, the tenants, and even the village. Its gentler rhythms filled my soul in a way that London never had. It was there that I began to know Zander's love—and where I would live out my life loving him in return.

He brushed an errant hair from my cheek. "You don't know how it makes me feel that you already call Goodwyn home." He swallowed against an emotion I'd not seen before. "I have been alone. Much alone."

"When can we leave?"

"Give me three more days?"

How quickly time passed. "Christmas season will be upon us in but the twinkling of an eye."

"Will it?"

"I daresay Goodwyn Abbey gets very cold in the winter." Would he grasp my subtlety?

"Yes, rather cold, I'm afraid."

I loved Zander—wanted him to know. "One might need help…warming up at night, I think."

The carriage stopped and the door flung open, giving him no chance to respond. I did not trust myself to look at him. How could I have embarrassed myself so completely? I ran to my bedroom and berated myself for sounding so wanton, even if he was my own dear husband.

The night had been a mixture of romance and shock. Of resolve and yet another nagging question. I'd ruined everything allowing my feelings to run away with me.

An hour after the maid left me with a hot cup of tea, a note slid silently beneath my door. A single sheet of paper in Zander's hand.

My Dearest Wife,

I'd never thought the impending winter season to be a blessing in disguise. If the bitter cold is what brings us to know the warmth of marriage, then let the winds blow. We will only draw closer and warmer. It cannot harm us when we are truly one.

We have each known the cold, too long absent of this kind of fire. All the more reason that I wish to love you full and well. That you will never have to question my heart, nor my constancy to you. I spoke my vows and I meant them—how much more I've come to revere and believe those vows since knowing that you are the all – and everything – my soul needs apart from God.

Do not be embarrassed, my love. It will be my honor to hold you each night for the rest of our days. I have waited for you alone.

Zander

P.S. Goodwyn Abbey is also rather cool in the summer. I will kiss you in the morning. Sleep, dearest.

If words might kindle fire, this one did. One I couldn't put out no matter how hard I tried. I did not wait for morning but found my way to his chamber and his arms before another long hour passed.

Chapter Twenty-Six

After many hours of travel, a night at the same inn we'd occupied after our wedding, we were finally home. *Home.*

We'd arrived rather late. Seeing Matthew would have to wait until morning. I stifled a laugh.

"What is it?" Zander's brow rose.

I stepped closer to the fire and shivered. "Cold, isn't it?"

"Oh?" He wrapped his arms around me and kissed my neck. "I'd say you're frozen through and through."

I looked up at him. "I don't want a separate chamber."

Something dropped to the floor and we both startled. Zander laughed. Nancy had walked into our parlor.

Zander nodded to her. "I'll get it, Nancy. Never mind that." She left us alone and I covered my eyes with my hands.

"I'm not the only one shocking the staff." He tugged at my hands. "At least word will spread that we are not to be disturbed. Come, don't hide."

I dropped my hands and leaned into his firm chest.

"Are you certain, Elaina?"

I lifted my face to his. "I find it hard to leave you."

"Then we shall simply make appropriate adjustments to the rooms. Meanwhile, yours..." he winked, "or mine?"

The next morning—or rather, late morning, we made our way down the hall to Matthew's room. I couldn't wait to see him.

But he wasn't there. The bed was rumpled and the doctor absent his post.

Zander tore down the steps and I followed as fast as I could. He shouted for the housekeeper and nearly the entire staff ran to assist. "Where is he? And Dr. Rillian? Answer me, now!"

My stomach squeezed. Surely, he wasn't gone. Surely, he'd not been taken from us.

The old housekeeper huffed. "Simmer down, Master Sherborne. You would raise the dead with that voice."

The butler bowed. "I believe, Lord and Lady Sherborne will find them out of doors."

"Out of doors? In this chill? The boy cannot walk. Where is Dr. Rillian?"

"With them, I believe."

Zander grabbed my hand and pulled me along behind him. "I'm sorry—I've never known Dr. Rillian to be so reckless."

We made our way outside and looked around the garden. Laughter rose from the stables, so we ran that direction.

I entered first. There was Callum, with Matthew in his arms, carrying him like a child. His wrapped legs held aloft, his broken arm held straight behind Callum's neck.

"Aye, Broonie, give him yer kisses. Show the boy love."

Matthew laughed, "She has many whiskers for a lady." He presented her with an apple and stroked her nose. "Maybe I'll be able to ride her someday."

"I believe you shall." The two turned at Zander's voice.

"Auntie! Lord Sherborne!" Matthew's eyes shone.

"I believe this young man has had enough of the cold for one day." Dr. Rillian patted Broonie's neck. "Much needed fresh air."

Callum carried him inside to the library where a cot had been set up. Dr. Rillian checked his pulse. "I'll give you some time to talk."

No sooner had the door closed than Matthew began. "Did you find the keys? What do they open? Why were they important to everyone?"

We spent the hour, explaining as best as we could. I couldn't keep Aunt Honora's passing a secret but how to explain her part? And his relation to her? Should I do so?

Zander believed that we should respect the man within him and tell the whole truth. We did not leave out a single detail. He took it hard, especially about Aunt Honora's death. How I wish I could have spared him.

When tears had dried and coffee had been delivered, Matthew relaxed against his pillow. I tried him. "Is there anything else you haven't told us? Anything at all?"

Matthew swallowed and shook his head. I wasn't convinced. He grew very quiet.

Zander leaned forward. "Did you know that I had guards placed around Goodwyn Abbey? And they are here still."

His eyes widened, as did mine.

"You are safe here. Nothing more will happen to you on my watch." Zander tried again. "Did you see something you weren't supposed to see or hear something you weren't meant to hear?"

Matthew sniffed as his face grew pale. He nodded.

"Can you tell us?"

"I lived in the caves for a few weeks. Only one cave was occupied. They were having a meeting."

"Who?"

"Men. And someone who looked rich and important."

"You heard what they said?"

"I did, but I didn't understand what they meant. When I was caught, I told them I wanted to find Uncle Carl. That's when they demanded the keys."

Zander nodded. "They somehow knew Carl didn't have them—and that you did."

Carl was the only one who knew Matthew had the keys. He had told them, but probably never imagined they would hurt Matthew—or even that he'd survived the wreck. They'd been looking for his body.

I looked to Zander and pressed on. "What were they talking about?"

"About weapons and delivering them to some mill before they were required for a rising between them and another one." He shook his head. "Made no sense. What is a rising?"

Zander looked at me then back at Matthew. "No, it makes perfect sense, given what we now know. The full word is *uprising*."

Carl was being manipulated into participating in an uprising? That explained a great deal. Zander sprang into action. Sent word immediately to the magistrate, constables, and runners.

The weeks that followed revealed much. Banbury's various locations along the coast had been discovered. The inns he frequented, things he'd left behind. A wealth of his devious master plans were revealed, including orchestrating an uprising between two competing mills. Twisted as he was, Banbury planned to watch the battle from the window of a nearby inn through a spyglass. He'd garner bets from the Ton. As though men's lives were but tin toys. These facts were discovered in a stack of letters he'd failed to burn before his unexpected death.

Matthew had heard and seen too much. He'd seen that Banbury, identified by his description, was the rich, important man at the meeting in the cave. Banbury had ordered his own grandson to be beaten and broken almost to the point of death. The brutes that worked for him had to prove themselves through violent obedience. What happened to Matthew would happen to anyone who disobeyed. But Banbury didn't know he'd attacked his own heir.

Indeed, Matthew would inherit every stick and stone left to the Banbury's tarnished name. Accounts untouched by crime. A massive estate but twenty miles from London. Everything would go to Matthew, except for Banbury's title as stated by the law. The news stunned. Though Matthew thought little of what was being handed to him. Such is justice – and irony.

I wondered what Aunt Honora would think were she still alive. Her rightful place within society finally regained? But I knew differently. She wouldn't have thrived under the weight of the scandal, nor would she have been happy. Between the Dawes downfall and the Banbury intrigue, his position would never be free of taint—until Matthew could prove himself a gentleman. A man standing on his own merit and goodness. And he would. I was sure of it.

Lady Banbury moved to a smaller estate she'd inherited from her mother's side of the family, and, I heard, refused to wear mourning dresses. Who could blame her? Most likely she felt only relief, not grief. Zander was legally appointed as guardian until Matthew came of age. A job he took with honor. Matthew would need every bit of training and education to be among the peerage...

Christmas was upon us. Matthew and I sat together threading brightly colored ribbons, reminiscing yuletides past. We decided to dwell on the good and often prayed together for Carl and his family. I wrote faithfully to Lyvia and was finally able to tell her the news of Matthew's discovery. Learning that, she finally responded.

Callum sat with us, folding and twisting old newspapers into his fanciful floral creations. How like God, I thought, able to turn bad news into something far better, more worthy, than I could have ever imagined. Something so beautiful—while the facts remained, words unchanged, yet we ourselves had. By faith and trust. A press and a new placement, a few necessary cuts. Callum handed me a rose with that bashful grin of his. Love that covered a multitude of sins.

Molly carried in a tray of hot Christmas punch as Zander returned from the village, with the vicar in tow. The Thomhows and their children were to join us for games and dinner.

A voice I hadn't heard for nearly five years rang out. "Elaina!" I rose from my chair and turned, hardly believing my ears.

"Caroline!" Oh, Caroline. My sister had come to me. How much I needed to see her again! The next few minutes were a blur of tears and embraces. Forgiveness flowed freely, my heart nearly burst.

When I had run through a good stack of handkerchiefs and shown my sister and her rather handsome husband to their room to refresh themselves before supper, I pulled my own husband close. "I love you, Zander."

He cupped my cheek with his hand and leaned his head against mine. "The vicar is watching us."

"Oh? Do you think he'll mind?"

Zander pressed a kiss to my lips. Then another.

The vicar whistled and clapped his hands. "Quite a performance, you two, but be aware that your other guests have arrived."

Callum giggled uproariously from the shadow of his corner.

For this grace, Lord, I thank thee...

Epilogue

Matthew was finally beginning to walk again when Carl's trial took place. The experience was difficult, but Zander declared that he acted the man's part and confessed, as he'd done before. Given the nature of the situation, the judge was fair. Merciful, even, for we thought Carl to likely hang. As the deaths were an indirect result of Banbury's schemes, it was decided that the Zephyr's captain should bear the brunt of the guilt, for it was he who made the final decision to allow his ship to sail into the rocks. The captain, though, had already paid with his life that fateful night. Carl would be sent to Australia and Lyvia and the children would go with him, to start a new life.

My last letter from Lyvia begged us to see them off. Before they sailed, we stood on the dock, embracing. I might never see her in this life again—or those precious children—but they would forever be in my heart.

Carl stood with his head down, his hat off. His scarred face wet with tears. I gave him my hand and he took it. We shared no words, but he knew. I forgave him. As God had given me grace to do.

They boarded the ship with a good summer breeze to send them swiftly away. I whispered a prayer for their safety. Zander tucked my hand within his arm and led me back to the waiting carriage. We would head home to Goodwyn for a few weeks, and then, to Scotland. To see Caroline...

So much joy, so much to be grateful for.

Acknowledgments

It is a truth I must universally acknowledge that without the Elinor Dashwood-sensibilities of my dear friend and critique partner, Danielle Grandinetti, I'd be lost. Thank you, friend, for prodding me to reach my goals to complete this trilogy even when I didn't think I could.

About the Author

Ann Elizabeth Fryer loves nothing more than using story and romance to relay the depths and graciousness of a Father who holds us securely in the palms of His hands. Ann, her husband, and three children make their home in small-town Illinois where they can hear church bells keep time and tradition.

The Hearts Unlocked Collection:
Of Needles and Haystacks
Of Horse and Rider
Of Hearts and Home
Of Time and Circumstance
Of Pens and Ploughshares
Butterton Brides Series:
A Convenient Sacrifice
A Favorable Match, coming November 2023
An Opportune Proposal, coming January 2024

Printed in Dunstable, United Kingdom